A
Harlequin
Romance

OTHER

Harlequin Romances

by ROUMELIA LANE

1180—ROSE OF THE DESERT
1212—HIDEAWAY HEART
1262—HOUSE OF THE WINDS
1290—A SUMMER TO LOVE
1338—SEA OF ZANJ
1395—TERMINUS TEHRAN
1479—THE SCENTED HILLS
1547—CAFÉ MIMOSA
1654—IN THE SHADE OF THE PALMS
1745—NURSE AT NOONGWALLA
1823—ACROSS THE LAGOON
1920—HARBOUR OF DECEIT

HARBOUR OF DECEIT

by

ROUMELIA LANE

HARLEQUIN BOOKS

TORONTO
WINNIPEG

Harlequin edition published October 1975
SBN 373-01920-3

Original hard cover edition published in 1975
by Mills & Boon Limited.

All the characters in this book have no existence outside the imagination of the Author, and have no relation whatsoever to anyone bearing the same name or names. They are not even distantly inspired by any individual known or unknown to the Author, and all the incidents are pure invention.

Printed in Canada

1920

CHAPTER ONE

THE loaded bus groaned its way along King Street and lurched unsteadily round the narrow turn into Barker's Row. Southampton was experiencing a drought and every shudder and drag of the bus wheels flung up the dust of weeks which had collected on the pavements and deposited it in gritty particles amongst the packed passengers inside.

Sarah gazed unflinchingly ahead beside the open windows. Strap-hanging along with a dozen or so other city office workers, she had none of their apathy at the thought of another Monday morning to be got through. As always she viewed the prospect of several hours shut away behind a desk wading through tedious papers with a clear eye and a determined keenness.

She was one of the first to alight where other buses were disgorging their passengers in the town centre, and leaving the early morning rush she made her way along a narrow lane behind the grey-stoned civic buildings. Her place of employment, Grapplewick, Grapplewick and Small Ltd., Marine Lawyers, was one of a line of antiquated offices built originally as a row of shops, but long since squashed into obscurity by the sprawling Victorian architecture.

If Sarah noticed the grime on the paintwork as she approached, the peeling gold lettering on the gaunt window-panes, she paid no attention to it, but stepped along purposefully to where a shaft of sunlight fell short of the dark open doorway. In the gloom inside the two junior office girls had their heads together as usual giving giggling whispered accounts of their romantic adventures over the weekend.

"Good morning, Miss Martindale." First one and then

the other piped up as they drew apart hurriedly and dived for their typewriters.

Sarah inclined them a nod in passing. She knew that their amused glances met behind her back and she heard their stifled titters following her. She accepted this as a natural hazard in making her way to her own desk at the far end of the room. She had no idea that to the girls she presented a rather contradictory picture. Severe in her fawn tweed suit, fawn hair hidden away beneath fawn cloche hat, she moved along with her brisk step, unaware that her curved hips swung provocatively.

Down in her own corner she removed her suit jacket, placed it on the faded satin hanger she had bought at a church summer sale several years before and taking off her hat settled down to work. She had barely got her papers sorted out when the bell rang summoning her to the main office. This was rather a nuisance, for she liked at least a half hour to arrange her desk. It was also most unusual for the senior member of the staff to be in his rooms so early. With a little frown of annoyance she picked up her pad and pencil and walked rapidly along the passageway towards the chambers at the back of the building.

Old Mr. Grapplewick was shuffling around near his bookcase when she entered his office. A rotund, doddering figure with a white dome of a head and a large double chin, he wore a pair of black-framed glasses half-way down his nose. These he was in the habit of ignoring completely, preferring to wheeze and grunt his gaze upwards over the top of them to see what was going on.

The pungent smell of dust and linseed, stale pipe smoke and old leather was so familiar to Sarah she had long since ceased to notice it. Pencil poised she was about to take her straight-backed chair at the side of the desk when Mr. Grapplewick, pretending he had only just noticed her, turned and waggled a finger at the padded leather chair opposite his.

As they exchanged good mornings Sarah placed her pad and pencil neatly on the desk, knowing they wouldn't be required. The fact that she had been offered the seat normally reserved for clients told her that she was in for one of Mr. Grapplewick's friendly chats which usually came up about this time each year. She sat down, stifling her impatience to get back to work.

Her employer fidgeted his way across the room lifting his eyebrows ponderingly over law books and peering at papers scattered about, wheezing breezily as he did so, "Uncommonly warm for this time of the year, eh, what! We'll suffer for all this sunshine, you mark my words."

Taking his time, he lowered his fat awkwardly into his chair and leaning back in customary pose, his fingers making a church steeple and his thumbs flubbering his double chins, he gave Sarah a contemplative look and asked amiably, "How long have you been with us now, Miss Martindale?"

"It will be ten years at the end of next week, Mr. Grapplewick," Sarah replied dutifully.

"Ah yes! I remember that nervous little sixteen-year-old who first came to us. Straight from school you were, and too afraid to come and collect your wages on Fridays, heh, heh . . ."

He gave his usual cracked chuckle and Sarah sat unblinkingly, knowing the form well. If his ramblings followed their normal course she could hope to be away in about ten minutes.

"Your father was alive then," Mr. Grapplewick reminisced as he always did about this time each year. "He was a fine man. We were in the Army together, you know." He brought his gaze down from the ceiling and eyed Sarah over the top of his glasses to reaffirm sympathetically, "You lost your mother when you were quite small, I believe?"

"That's right, Mr. Grapplewick," Sarah replied in her usual correct manner. She sat up straight and waited for her employer to continue. Eventually, after tapping his finger tips lightly together and musing over her benevolently, he meandered on, "Are you still living in the little flat your father bought in the Bellminster building? Such a small place, I always thought, for the two of you."

"I'm still there," Sarah nodded with a patience she had developed down the years. She smiled as she always did, "The rooms *are* a little cramped, but I'm very comfortable."

She waited, poised, ready to leave, knowing the end of the interview off by heart. Mr. Grapplewick would ask her if she were happy working for the firm and she would say that she was. Then they would shake hands across the desk and with the annual good-will chat behind her she would be free to get on with her day's work.

She had already taken herself off mentally and was making notes in her mind concerning the paperwork on her desk when Mr. Grapplewick, viewing her over the top of his glasses, suddenly swerved from routine and asked her smilingly, "Have you ever been abroad, Miss Martindale?"

Battling with her irritation at this unexpected turn in the conversation, Sarah answered a little shortly, "Once or twice. My Father liked Italy for his holidays. Then there was the office trip two or three years back."

"Ah yes, our week-end in Paris. Quite a success, our little outing, if I remember rightly." Mr. Grapplewick resisted the urge to float off reminiscently again and began to shuffle and move things around on his desk. His actions to Sarah seemed a trifle nervous, though he retained his friendly air.

Leafing through a phone file which, as it turned out, had nothing at *all* to do with the conversation, he said jovially after some moments had elapsed, "There's a small job I'd like you to do for me, Miss Martindale."

As his gaze travelled back to the clients' chair Sarah lowered a glance pointedly at her watch. *Now* what was he going to ask her to do? Pay the office electricity bill at the town hall? Or research through old records at the library? It was bound to be one of those annoying little tasks that would put her hopelessly behind schedule for the rest of the morning.

Unbending, she listened as Mr. Grapplewick told her, "We're expecting some important documents down from London some time this morning. They are required urgently by the Portuguese partner of Carvalho and Hunt, growers and shippers of port wine, who are clients of ours. I want you to catch the afternoon plane and deliver them to Senhor Carvalho at his estate in the Amorida Valley district."

The afternoon *plane*! *Portuguese* partner! Sarah shook herself, afraid that she wasn't properly awake. She scraped together her full attention, urged closer to the desk and said with a watery, questioning smile, "I'm sorry, Mr. Grapplewick. For a moment I thought you were asking me to go to Portugal."

"That's right, Miss Martindale." Though he was still smiling Mr. Grapplewick's manner became a little brusque. He rose and fidgeted about the room, adding in pleasant but unmistakable tones of dismissal, "You can carry on as normal this morning. I'll inform you when the documents arrive."

Sarah, sitting rigid, stayed where she was. "Go to Portugal? Me?" A surge of angry colour stained her throat as she eyed her employer. She replied caustically, "I'd really rather not, if you don't mind."

"Now, now, Miss Martindale." Mr. Grapplewick dropped his benign employer role and assumed as his right, as he always did when things weren't going well, a tetchy and dogmatic attitude. "This is no time to get difficult. I'm too old to make the trip myself and there's no one else I can spare in the office at the moment. Besides, it's all arranged." His pettish tones brooked no argument. "Webster, my chauffeur, has instructions to drive you to the airport. He'll stop at your flat on the way so that you can pick up a few things." Mr. Grapplewick turned away. Acting nervously again, he began to hunt busily for some vague requirement, making a fidgety show of sounding offhand as he added, "I should pack a sizeable suitcase if I were you. The Carvalho estate is a little out of the way, I believe."

Tight-lipped, Sarah rose and walked with a suffering air to the door. Outside she let her annoyance have free rein. Fly off to Portugal indeed! Just like that! Didn't the man know that such a trip would play havoc with her typing schedule? It looked as though she was going to be allowed little time to get on with it this morning, and he seemed to think that she wouldn't manage to get back before tomorrow, so that would be another day lost.

Snorting with frustration at the inconvenience, she marched back to her desk and tried to organise her thoughts. But it was impossible to settle down to anything properly with all this upset which had been calmly foisted upon her. She spent the morning picking irritably at odd papers and hoping that the documents wouldn't turn up, or that some other more suitable courier had been found to deliver them.

At two o'clock, just after lunch, when she was summoned once again to the senior partner's office, she knew that no one had.

Mr. Grapplewick was conveniently absent from behind his desk. It was Webster, a grizzle-haired, taciturn figure in grey uniform, who handed Sarah her instructions and her air ticket together with the documents in a large flat envelope. The two of them went out through the private entrance into the street where Mr. Grapplewick's dignified old Wolseley was waiting.

Sarah sat glancing out of the windows as the car shunted through heavy traffic, bitterly envious of the bustling people in the city. Unlike her they had been left to get on with the work of the day uninterrupted. At her flat the car waited while she collected some things. In her bedroom she moved crossly from drawer to drawer. How she hated these last-minute arrangements. How could she think clearly with so little time?

At her wits' end, she opened a suitcase and flung in an assortment of odds and ends which she probably wouldn't need anyway. Then there were the windows to see to. As she wouldn't be home tonight she would have to go round and lock each one. What a nuisance! Feeling thoroughly ruffled by the time she had completed all the little tasks, she tugged up her suitcase and locking up behind her went out to the car.

It was a dreary ride to the airport. She had done it once or twice before and found no joy in gazing at sprawling industrial buildings and fields of tenement blocks. Webster pulled in at the parking lot beside the airstrip and carried her suitcase to the airport lounge. After that she was on her own. He drove away without a backward glance, leaving her to make what she could of the voice booming out indistinctly over the loudspeakers.

In no mood to care whether she caught her plane or not, Sarah bought a paperback with an historical background from the nearby bookstall and found an armchair. But for a helpful stewardess checking on air tickets she might have read on without hearing the urgent summons directed at her and other lackadaisical passengers still wanted for the Portugal flight.

With a resigned air she rose. Her suitcase was checked in and along with the other stragglers she made her way out to the plane.

Once they were airborne Sarah decided that there was little point in shirking the issue any longer. She had been given a job to do and the conscientious streak in her demanded that she do it well. Discarding the paperback, she opened the large envelope on her knee and spent the time familiarising herself with its contents.

Besides the documents, stitched in an opaque plastic bag, there was a quantity of Portuguese currency, and several pages of precise instructions on how to reach the Carvalho estate, apparently an isolated grape-growing concern situated deep in the Amorida Valley. She was informed as she read the instructions that there should be little problem with the language, because most of the people in the port wine country knew a smattering of English. But in case of difficulty a pocket phrase book had been included. Sarah skimmed through the pages of weird words, hoping she would never have to use it.

It was after six when the plane banked in over the sea and landed at the airport outside Porto. According to Sarah's information this was an industrial city and centre of the wine industry. And it was from here that she would have to take a bus to the little harbour town of Laso, the nearest point to her destination inland.

After the bustle through the Customs she made her way out into the dusk-veiled evening. She hadn't intended to pay any attention to her surroundings. After all, her job was simply to deliver the documents and then catch the next plane back. However, the bracing sea air laced with the scents of mimosa and eucalyptus startled her a little, and she wasn't prepared for the violet-tinted hills and the deep afternoon blue of the sky.

Keeping her mind on her work, she hailed a taxi. She took care to observe that it was a metered cab and that the meter was turned down before they started out. None of this was in her instructions, but Sarah practised a natural astuteness in situations of this kind.

As soon as the taxi driver learned that she wanted the bus station for Laso he was all for driving her to the harbour town himself. He could do it cheap, very cheap, he pointed out in his atrocious English. For only ninety escudos! He scribbled the figure down and showed it to her proudly. Sarah glanced at the notepad with disdain. She happened to know that the bus fare was less than a quarter of the price he quoted and she saw no sense in squandering the firm's money. Though the man grinned and pleaded to be allowed the luxury of earning for himself a leisurely ride Sarah held out firmly for the bus station.

Good-naturedly he drew up there and swung Sarah's suitcase out beside her in the small deserted square. She checked with the meter carefully and handed him a sensible but not exorbitant tip. Then she turned briskly away to find her point of departure.

There was one woman, black-shawled and aloof, waiting beside the Laso indicator. Later an old man in black beret and ill-matched jacket and trousers came to join them. Sarah glanced frequently at her watch. How she hated hanging about. A light here and there twinkled on in the houses bordering the square. Surely the bus would come soon?

To pass the time she let her gaze roam indifferently over the little church across the space, white and simple, and the haphazard steps and gateways of the crowded dwellings. All at once, its roaring, clattering engine shattering the silence of the square, a vintage yellow bus came tearing round the side of the church and shrieked to a halt at the Laso stop.

Its appearance seemed to wake up the whole neighbourhood. People rushed from nowhere to climb aboard as the doors hissed open, colliding with those who were trying to get off. Not one to panic under normal circumstances, Sarah found herself hopping about uncertainly. She had had no time to read the front indicator and there was no one in authority whom she could ask. And the wretched vehicle was getting all set to shoot away again.

"Laso?" she enquired politely at the tumbling stream of humanity falling on to the pavement. Men in working clothes gave her blank smiles, and women in headscarves stared at her pityingly. She glanced about helplessly as the knot of people diminished and caught the steady gaze of the aloof black-shawled woman.

"Laso? *Nao*." The woman shook her head emphatically.

The man in the black beret also still waiting held up the fingers of his hands helpfully. "*Dez minutos.*"

Another ten minutes? Still unsure, Sarah watched the bus hurtle away.

The dour black-shawled woman surprised her by suddenly breaking out into an animated conversation with the old man. He in turn showed that behind the craggy, forbidding exterior lurked a sunny nature. They laughed and chatted amicably together, their friendly exchanges sounding strange to Sarah's ears.

After a few minutes she was subjected to another whirlwind arrival of Portuguese transport. Locked in the crush, in which her two companions boarded the bus, she gripped her suitcase and searched their faces hopefully.

"Laso? *Nao*," she was told sympathetically. While she struggled disbelievingly the doors hissed to in her face and she was left standing on the pavement.

The alighted passengers melted into the twilight. Worriedly Sarah looked at her watch and in doing so almost missed the arrival of the Laso bus. It was a deep, rich red colour and displayed its destination prominently in the front window.

Sarah stepped forward with relief, scolding herself for feeling unsure. Of course it was all right. Everything would go smoothly if she would just let herself relax.

The coach was almost full. As it lurched to a start she found a well at the back to place her suitcase and chose a seat nearby so that she could keep an eye on it. The ticket conductor, a youthful figure in a pale rumpled uniform, made his way down the long aisle towards her. He didn't like the five-hundred-escudo note she handed him. Politely he went off to get more change and came back with her ticket costing a mere twenty-two escudos. Sarah tucked it away carefully with her change in the pocket of her handbag and arranging the document envelope safely on her lap beneath it settled back, briskly content. All had seemed confusion back there, but now she could rest at ease. Her mission was well on the way to being accomplished.

She even had time to let her glance wander casually around the bus. It was very noisy. Everybody was chattering to someone else across the seats and people called to one another down the aisle. It was rather like a mobile party gathering. A group of swarthy-faced men who laughed and talked, showing yellow-stained teeth, wore neat suits and white shirts and tall-crowned black fedora hats.

The scenery outside of quaint houses lining the road spun leisurely by. Sarah moulded herself into her seat in anticipation of the journey. But they had only been travelling a few minutes when the bus stopped. The men in the black fedoras trooped out. Further along the road they drew up again to pick up a motley group including some youths smelling strongly of sea water and salt spray, and clutching fishing rods and the afternoon's catch in plastic bags.

As they joined the noisy throng Sarah watched the doors swish to with impatient satisfaction. Now that they had got practically a full load again perhaps they could get on to Laso. But no. She couldn't believe it when the bus pulled up again after going only a few yards, this time to let off a couple of basket-carrying housewives.

She had noticed the white push-button bells above the seats, and learned with a sinking feeling as they progressed that the passengers were at liberty to request a stop whenever they felt like it. Outside in the evening light red-roofed houses were scattered in a constant trickle over the countryside. Obviously every one of their occupants made use of this bus service along the road.

Mothers clutching children flagged it down at lonely intersections. Workmen and afternoon shoppers crowded the pavements of small hamlets at its approach. The driver was a cheerful sort, and pulled up jovially every time. Everyone knew him by name and jokes were exchanged as passengers came and went. Apparently riding a bus in Portugal was a social occasion. Sarah was the only one who was not enjoying the experience.

She fell into the practice of counting the moments tensely each time they got under way, willing the bus to cover a mile or two before something happened to stop it. Invariably when they had just picked up speed an arm would come up and tinkle the bell or someone would step out on the road ahead.

The handle of the clock at the front of the coach dragged round. The fishing youths whooped at and embarrassed every young girl who passed outside the windows or moved down the aisle, until they in turn came to their stop and tumbled out. Sarah began to see why the ticket conductor had looked down his nose at her five-hundred-escudo note, and why everyone had eyed her strangely when she had asked for Laso. It was obvious that no one travelled farther than the neighbouring hamlet or homestead along this coast road. Laso, the end of the line, might have been China to them for all they knew of it.

As the coach drew in for yet another change of passengers it became increasingly clear to Sarah that out of all those who had boarded at the start, only she and the driver and his mate would complete the journey. According to her information the distance was fifty kilometres. She looked at her watch and discovered with grim amusement that they were averaging a stop a minute. At this rate the journey of an hour was likely to take two.

Much to her intense discomfort her reckoning turned out to be about right. Just a little short of that time the bus ambled into its destination. It was by now hopelessly dark. There was nothing to be seen outside except a few sombre harbour buildings and the black oily gleam of water beyond a nearby wharf. A single street lamp lit the way dimly.

Welcoming the salt-laced air in her lungs after the stale ride, Sarah stepped down from the bus and struck out purposefully into the town, though she had no idea what she intended to do. Shattered by the trip, she couldn't see herself travelling another thirty odd kilometres out to the Carvalho estate tonight. Nor could she be sure that her arrival would be entirely convenient at so late an hour. As she thought about it, a weariness slowing her steps, she decided that though it was certainly a nuisance it might be better to stay the night in Laso and deliver the documents first thing in the morning.

Yes, that would appear to be the most sensible arrangement. Her aching bones in full agreement with the decision, she looked around hopefully as she walked. Everywhere was in darkness. But having made up her mind, she had no intention of being deterred by appearances. Ahead was a kind of café establishment with a dull glow coming from the windows and one or two tables and chairs lining the shadowy pavement.

Her brisk, matter-of-fact self again, she approached the figure slouched in the doorway and enquired crisply, "Hotel, *por favor*?"

After all, it was a common enough request in anybody's language.

The man tossed his cigarette away and gave her a smile showing that he possessed no teeth. " 'Ot—el? *Sim, senhora.*" He nodded and stepping out beckoned her to follow him. He would have taken her suitcase, but Sarah hung on tightly to it. Oh no! She had heard of people losing their luggage in this way. Ignoring the man's gesture, she made it perfectly clear by her expression that she was well aware of all the pitfalls of foreign travel.

He took her down past the side of the café and along a succession of dimly-lit narrow alleys. Sarah followed a few steps behind. Her heart beat a little faster when she viewed the rough clothes and rolling gait of her guide. The sound of his and her footsteps were thrown back from pale cottage walls and shuttered exteriors as they walked. Then rounding a corner they came out into a well-lit open space.

There were trees and a central strip of ornamental gardens, and one or two shops together with the odd pavement café were still doing business. Feeling better, Sarah let her gaze wander to where a tastefully-lit entrance showed one or two expensive cars parked at the front. Her guide led the way and gestured grandly, " 'Ot—el."

Pleased but taking care not to show it, Sarah opened her handbag and chose a coin. "*Obrigado.*" She thanked the man, and was surprised to see him back away, embarrassed at the offer of a tip. She remained steady. Well, he might have his pride, but she had hers too. "Take it." Standing no nonsense, she pressed the money into his hand. He gave her a gummy smile and touching his cap sloped off into the darkness.

Gripping her suitcase firmly, Sarah made her way to where the rose glow was streaming out into the night. Though all was peaceful in the tiny square there was something of a pandemonium going on inside the hotel. The first thing that struck Sarah was its compactness, just an elegant reception desk in the corner of a postage-stamp lounge. The second was the clutter of luggage which littered the way and cascaded over everything. All of the masculine type, it consisted of heavy duty travelling bags, stained and frayed with wear, odd-looking black boxes, a jumble of leather-cased equipment and rubber suits, the kind that men wore for diving.

Across the room was what appeared to be a small bar and circulating in and around the entrance were the obvious owners of the clutter, a husky group of individuals who threw back their drinks, slapped each other and guffawed loudly. More cars drew up outside. From the bar Sarah caught snatches of bawdy English conversation. As the men drifted out, briefly checked their equipment, then took themselves off laughingly past the desk, she kept her sedate gaze riveted on the clerk behind it and spoke up crisply above the din. "I'd like a room for one night."

The young man with dark eyes and pale slim hands

lifted his shoulders and said with an apologetic smile, *"Completo. Desculpe-me."*

Now what did that mean? Preferring to get by without the firm's phrase book, Sarah persisted firmly, "A single room, if you please. With a bath, if that's possible."

The clerk gazed about him helplessly and looking up from where he was checking figures in a ledger, a well-dressed elderly man, probably the manager, rose and told her in perfect English with a friendly gleam, "I regret, madam, the hotel is full."

Jaded, Sarah wouldn't let herself believe such unpleasant news. She said above the ribald humour at her back, "But you must have something?"

The manager was sympathetic but emphatic as he shook his head. He shrugged a glance over the piles of luggage and the departing figures making for the outdoors. "All the rooms have been taken by these men." He couldn't resist a twinkle of satisfaction as he told her, "We have never had so many guests all at one time. I believe they have come to do some surveying in the area."

Sarah pressed her lips together. Well, that was all very well for them. But what about her? She asked crossly, "Is there another hotel nearby?"

The manager eyed her as though she had said something amusing. "This is the *only* hotel," he told her, smiling. "Laso is a simple town with little to attract the tourist. Small as we are, we are seldom ever full up."

"But you are tonight," Sarah said testily. Silently cursing the overgrown schoolboys jostling each other in the doorway, she asked, "What about other types of accommodation?"

The reply from behind the desk was not heartening. "There is a *pensao* out on the road to Aguias."

A pension! Out of town! Refusing to even consider the idea, Sarah said flatly though with a note of desperation in her voice, "I've come all the way from Porto. I couldn't walk another step."

She didn't know whether the manager was familiar with the rigours of the bus journey or what, but he looked at her searchingly, then turned and spoke to the clerk. For several moments they rattled away together in Portuguese and Sarah listened to the strange-sounding language. Then the clerk hurried away and the manager turned and said kindly, "Perhaps we will think of something. It will be a small room, you understand, not normally used for guests. But for one night I think we can manage."

Sarah sagged with relief. She replied levelly, "I'm very grateful."

"Wait and we will see what we can do." With his friendly gleam the manager returned to his work.

Left on her own, Sarah had time to view the antics of the men over in the doorway. They seemed to have met up with others outside and were all congregating around a figure who had just emerged from a polished car. There was no doubt as-to this man's status, for all attention was directed his way as he stood chatting leisurely on the pavement. And above the complaints, bawdy jokes and expansive comments laid on for his benefit, a loud voice pleaded, "Hey, boss! Can't we run over to Porto? This town's got about as much life in it as Rip Van Winkle's grandmother!"

Everyone guffawed their agreement with the ribald remark, which also brought a lazy smile to the lips of the central figure. Feeling safe in her shadowy spot beyond the reception desk inside, Sarah eyed the man critically. He was as rugged as the rest of his team, but his suit was well cut and he wore an unmistakable air of authority. Sarah noted his smile, but she didn't share his humour. With something of a glare she was wondering sourly why he couldn't have waited one more night before taking over the town, when the desk clerk returned from his trip into the interior of the hotel.

He looked pleased, and conversed in low tones with his superior, after which he beckoned Sarah to follow him.

Carrying her own suitcase through a discreet entrance to one side of the desk, she tried not to notice that they were making for the kitchens. The steamy smell of cooking vegetables drifted along the passageway. In the dim distance the clatter of pans rose above coarse voices and laughter.

Where food cartons were piled high and tea towels hung limply on a makeshift line Sarah was shown into a room which appeared to be used mainly for storage. Stacked against the walls were discarded standard lamps, broken stools, and dressing tables and chairs in need of repair. In the only clear space available a small bed had been dragged into position and hastily made up with clean linen. A freshly laundered towel and bar of soap lay on the pillow.

Realising dismally that this was the best she could expect, Sarah dropped her suitcase. She looked round for a wash-basin and as though reading her mind the young night-receptionist hurriedly guided her into the doorway and pointed sheepishly along the passageway. Sceptically Sarah peered into the gloom.

Preparing to bolt back to his work, as he sensed her chilly approval of the arrangement, the young man informed her with a nervous smile, "*Preparada rapidamente alguma coisa para comer.*"

Sarah had an idea he was talking about food, but she was too tired to work it out. She closed the door after his departure and turned to her suitcase. Luckily she had thought to throw in a cotton housecoat. It was a relief to slip out of her clothes and fasten the light garment around her. Of course there were no coat hangers, so she had to drape her things over the jumble around the room; her suit jacket over a three-legged chair, and her skirt by its waist tapes from the knobs of an upturned drawer. Her hat she perched on the broken bracket of a bedside lamp.

For several moments after that she listened with her ear close to the door to the distant sounds of the kitchens. Somewhere out there was a wash-room and somehow she had to get to it without being noticed. Picking up the soap and towel, she took the plunge. There was only one dim electric light bulb screwed into the wall of the passageway, which was fine for keeping to the shadows but not so good for avoiding dangerous pantry impedimenta blocking the way. She stubbed her toe on an old fruit crate and almost toppled a half-used sack of potatoes.

A cool breeze guided her and eventually she came to an opening which looked on to a dark outside courtyard. On an old ill-fitting door out there she could just make out the lettering which someone had daubed in white paint, *Casa de Banho*. In a flash she was across the space and inside.

The whitewashed walls and crude fitments lit up garishly by a bare light bulb told her at once that she was sharing the kitchen staff facilities. And there wasn't even any hot water! In dark mood, she sluiced down as best she could, obtaining little lather and cursing the scum, later drying off briskly with the hotel towel. Then with her hair damp around her face she clutched her housecoat close at her throat and prepared for the dash back to her poky quarters.

She was looking out to see if the coast was clear when a sound across the yard made her shoot back inside the wash-room and clap the door shut to within an inch of her nose. With palpitating heart she listened to the slur of footsteps. Close at hand a voice grunted out a remark of some kind and this was followed by a bellow of laughter. Through the crack in the door she could see a brilliant shaft of light flooding the courtyard and framed against the interior bustle of the kitchens lounged a man of huge proportions. He wore a white apron round his tremendous girth and tilted over his black-bearded features was a chef's tall white hat.

Trapped, Sarah stood in the darkness champing on her frustration. She didn't see how she could possibly float past such a figure dressed as she was. Feeling a complete fool, she hung about, her nose glued to the gap in the door, waiting for an opportunity. The man was having a desultory conversation with someone inside. Occasionally he tossed a throaty remark over his shoulder and from somewhere beyond the blue smoke of something cooking came a laughing rejoinder.

Sarah marked time with her feet impatiently. It was growing chilly. A cool wind was wafting under the door, making her more and more aware of her flimsy apparel. At last her tormentor stirred himself from his lounging position and moved out into the night. For one awful moment Sarah thought he was heading her way. Then he tossed away the cigarette he had been smoking, turned inside and slammed the door shut behind him.

All was now pitch black. Struggling to readjust to the gloom, Sarah stumbled out of her hiding place and fled along the peril-strewn passageway back to safety. When she arrived at the lumber room her heart was banging as though she had run a mile. In a foul mood after the episode, she discovered that someone had paid a visit to her makeshift quarters while she had been away. One of the tottering dressing tables had been cleared of junk and on it was a food tray.

Sarah didn't doubt that the meal had been perfectly eatable when it had been placed there. Unfortunately because of her enforced stay in the wash-room everything was now stone cold. In a depressed state, she sat on the edge of the bed and picked her way through the congealed dishes. She coldly ignored the carafe of wine placed at the side of the tray, but thanked heaven for an apple for dessert to take the place of a toothbrush. Nothing would induce her to make another trip to the wash-room tonight!

The light in the room was very bright, probably to allow for workmen coming in to do furniture repairs. In one wall a column of frosted window reached from the ceiling down to the floorboards. Though street sounds could be heard coming from it Sarah had paid no particular attention to the window. What drew her notice to it, just as she was getting ready to climb into bed, was her sudden awareness of voices immediately outside.

Tensing, she paused in the task of running a comb through her hair. She was rapidly coming to the conclusion that the window faced directly on to the pavement and was but a stone's throw from the entrance to the hotel. She recognised the bawdy chatter of the surveyors, and to her horror she could make out quite clearly the masculine shapes on the other side of the frosted glass. Her heart leapt into her throat. If she could see them so plainly what could *they* see inside the room!

Seized with panic, she hopped about in her nightdress, trying to keep as far from the window as possible and at the same time looking for something to drape across it. Seeing the towel, she snatched it up and screening herself behind it clapped it against the glass. It was the feat of a contortionist trying to hold it there while she raked around with her feet for her shoes to weight it in position at the half-way ledge of the window.

When it was fixed she fell back panting on the bed, partly with exertion, and partly with a temper which was fast becoming frayed at the edges. She had had about as much as she could stand of full hotels and obnoxious males. Tomorrow, thank heavens, she would be on her way back to England.

She crept gingerly past the towel and went to put the light out. But if she thought she was going to settle down to sleep she was mistaken. The noise of slamming of car doors and shouts of laughter soon put paid to that. It appeared that the odious men hadn't gone to Porto after all but were making a night of it between the hotel and the cafes in the square. Grimly Sarah lay for long enough listening to their antics. She wished their precious boss would come along and round them up. Thinking of that laconic figure she had seen earlier in their midst made her turn and flounce up her pillow sourly. But for *him* she could be sleeping in a comfortable room now instead of bedding down like a fugitive somewhere inside the bowels of the hotel.

CHAPTER TWO

It was the early hours before peace came to the square. Sarah didn't remember dropping off, nor did she hear much until the morning sunshine flooded in through the frosted window. She stirred herself finally, vaguely aware that there had been a phantom visit to her door some minutes earlier. And sure enough, when she looked out a cup of coffee on the draughty floor was rapidly gathering a skin on top.

Resignedly Sarah pulled it in and gulped it down. There was little hope now of finding comfort until she was back on the plane, so the sooner she completed her mission the better. Thank goodness she had plenty of freshening-up pads in her handbag, and these she used lavishly, enjoying the tingle of lavender on her skin in the place of soap and water.

She dressed quickly and squashed her hat into place with the help of a cracked mirror. Thanks to the nocturnal caperings of the surveyors she had risen much later than she had intended. She packed her nightclothes and oddments and snapping her case shut swung out of the room. It was no easy matter finding her way back along the cluttered corridor, but carefully avoiding the route to the kitchens she finally came to the door that led out into the hotel lounge. And there was the reception desk.

As she might have expected, there was no sign of the night receptionist and the young daytime desk clerk knew nothing at all about her improvised sleeping arrangements. In fact Sarah doubted if he knew anything of last night's noisy upheaval which had shaken the hotel, for all was now peaceful. In the orderly atmosphere one could even hear the ponderous ticking of the lounge clock.

Fortunately the young man spoke English, so all she

had to do was explain what had happened. It was easy to see that the occasions on which a guest was thrust into an oddments room alongside the kitchens were rare, for the desk clerk seemed totally unable to grasp the situation. Sarah felt her frustration building up again. If no one knew about her night's stay how could she pay her bill? She was too busy trying to get this point through to the young man to give any attention to the sound of firm footsteps which came across the lounge, passed the desk and went outside.

The clerk listened with a worried smile to her ramblings, then decided to hurry away to seek advice at a higher level and Sarah was left tapping her foot impatiently beside the desk. When he returned, however, having apparently winkled out the manager from some corner of the hotel, all was in order. With a smile he promptly made her out a bill, and Sarah was pleasantly surprised to see that it was for a negligible amount. Well, that would be a saving of the firm's money anyway, she thought with begrudging satisfaction.

She paid up and picking up her luggage went out. The tiny square had a workaday bustle about it. Shops and cafés were opening up and cotton-shirted road-sweepers dodged between the trickle of traffic. There was no sign of the cluster of cars parked last night outside the hotel.

Sarah looked about her, but decided quickly against enquiring about public transport to take her out to the Amorida Valley district. She couldn't stand a repeat of yesterday afternoon's performance. A dreary bus ride—oh no! Also the new day made her think of the offices of Grapplewick, Grapplewick and Small, and the work that would be piling up on her desk. If she didn't get back soon, heaven knew what chaos she would find. Recklessly, considering it would cost four or five times more than the bus fare, she hailed a lonely taxi parked by the curb.

The driver was a little confused at first, but once Sarah got him to understand that she did indeed want him to drive her all the way out to the Amorida Valley vineyards, a distance of thirty miles or so, he gladly set about the task of taking her there. He knew the Carvalho Estate well—Quinta da Amorida, he called it—so there was nothing to do but sit back and wait until they arrived.

In between fretting about the dreadful waste of time Sarah gave half an eye to the scenery. Out of Laso the countryside was very green and hilly. Later there were twisting gorges and occasionally a river could be seen cutting between the pine-clad slopes.

Impatiently Sarah kept an eye open for the Carvalho house. It appeared that the land the family owned was extensive, for long after the car had passed the marking of the boundaries there was nothing but mile upon mile of vineyards. Then she saw the Quinta in the distance, red-roofed and impressive and screened by waving poplars and willows. At last! She breathed a sigh of relief. Her job was almost finished.

As they drew near she saw that the house was walled in like a fortress amidst the surrounding tiers of grapevines. Great wrought iron gates faced one on the approach. But the taxi driver seemed familiar with the procedure for entering. He got out and pulled a bell at the side. Within a few minutes the gates were opened by an unseen hand and they were driving through grounds laid out like a small village, with winery buildings and work-sheds very much in evidence. Later formal gardens pointed the way to the house. The taxi driver parked under a laurel tree and Sarah told him to wait. She was hoping her business wouldn't take long, for she was all too aware of the meter ticking over.

The house had a rich yet antiquated appearance, its heavily carved window frames and doors contrasting darkly with the cream walls. As Sarah approached the wide steps flanked by flowering shrubs a figure came down them towards her.

"Ah, Miss Martindale. At last you have arrived!" As a

hand was held out towards her Sarah saw a slightly built elderly man, impeccably dressed, with greyish receding hair and a pleasant countenance. With shrewdly twinkling eyes he looked past her as he shook her hand. "You have a bag? Ah yes." And in his cultured English he proceeded rapidly to have it brought inside.

A little alarmed, Sarah watched him pay off the taxi driver and send him on his way. She hoped Senhor Carvalho realised she would need alternative transport to get back to Laso.

Expansively he led her inside. She received a vague impression of a spacious hall with high-hanging chandelier and surrounding dark alcoves, before being shown into a tastefully furnished room with cherry walls and white paintwork. Rich gold-framed pictures hung on the walls.

Senhor Carvalho eyed the plastic package she held tightly in her hand. "You've brought the deeds. Good," he said. And with a cordial smile. "You'd like a little refreshment. Tea perhaps?"

"That would be nice." Sarah allowed herself a few moments to relax. After all, her job was almost finished now and she had had nothing this morning except a cup of cold coffee. A maid who had followed them into the doorway was dispatched with a lengthy order in Portuguese. She closed the door as she went out.

Senhor Carvalho hovered expectantly. Sarah stood unblinkingly with her precious merchandise. She had never done this kind of thing before, but she knew how to proceed. Holding on to the documents, she faced the smiling man and asked with businesslike cool, "Have you some form of identification?"

The dark eyes of her host showed a flicker of amusement. "Well . . . I think my ancestors would vouch for me if they could speak . . ." With a glint of suppressed humour he waved an arm at the dark painted portraits on the wall. "And look!" As though he had just thought of it he pulled out a gold watch from his waistcoat pocket and flicked open the front. "Here is a gift I received last birthday."

Looking past him at the watch, Sarah peered close and carefully examined the scroll lettering. The inscription was in Portuguese but she could make out the name *Alberto Gonzalez de Carvalho*. Well, that ought to be enough, she supposed. She had to have some proof, of course. It would be very bad to come all this way and then deliver the documents into the wrong hands. She scrutinised the amused countenance of the man before her while she considered, then deciding it was all right she handed over the packet.

"Thank you . . ." As he took the deeds from her Senhor Carvalho hesitated and eyeing her with a probing twinkle he queried, "You *are* Miss Martindale?"

Sarah smiled. She knew he was teasing her now. The maid knocked and entered with a laden tray and as it was set down Sarah's host beckoned her to the chair beside it. "Please help yourself to anything you wish." He went over to the window to break the plastic seal on the documents.

The armchair was very comfortable. Sarah poured herself tea from the big silver tea-pot and spooned in sugar from the matching silver bowl. A delicately embossed plate held a round of wafer-thin sandwiches, and another was starred with tiny Portuguese pastries. A couple of sandwiches, to Sarah's mind, would sustain her until she got back to Laso.

As she ate her gaze wandered idly to Senhor Carvalho over by the window. She noticed the shrewd glint back in his eyes as he painstakingly perused the documents she had brought, and the mouth that she felt was accustomed to smiling had tightened and was drawn down slightly at the edges.

She finished her second cup of tea just as he came to the end of the small print and locking the deeds away, genial once again, he moved towards her. "You are feeling better after your long journey?" He smiled encouragingly.

"Good! Now you must come and see the winery."

Sarah's heart dropped. She hadn't planned on doing any sightseeing. Time was passing on and she had to get back to the offices in Southampton. However, Senhor Carvalho obviously felt he owed her the courtesy of showing her around. This made it difficult for her to explain that she would much rather be getting on her way. All she could do was humour the man, who really was quite charming, and get it over with as quickly as possible.

Nodding in agreement, she rose and allowed him to lead the way. They went across the hall, which now seemed enormous, and out of an open door framing a view of rising terraced vineyards and blue sky. Senhor Carvalho chatted to her as they made their way through a walled-in courtyard draped with hanging flower-pots and out across a space of beaten earth towards the estate buildings.

If Sarah had wanted to she could have learned all about the making of port wine as the facts and figures of picking and processing, new wine pressing methods and storing facilities were explained to her. But she gave only half an ear to her host's conversation in between stealing surreptitious glances at her wristwatch. She saw sheds lined with enormous oaken casks and others where spanking new machinery stood beside the old treading tanks.

"Many people are sad that the bare feet no longer tread." Senhor Carvalho gave a philosophical shrug, "But we must move with the times."

In a building where the walls were thick and pitted with age he waved an arm. "This is the kitchen we maintain for our seasonal workers." Sarah couldn't help staring at a gargantuan stove about the size of a small car. A crane supported huge cauldrons, each holding a paddle to stir the food.

Under a leafy loggia adjoining the kitchen they passed rows of neatly stacked baskets used for carrying the grapes. "After being pressed and casked," Senhor Carvalho explained, guiding her out into the sunshine again, "the port wine goes by road to our blending and ageing warehouses at Laso harbour."

As they turned back towards the house Sarah had the feeling that this last remark was meant to hold some special significance, though concerning what she couldn't have said. Nor was she particularly interested. *She* wasn't in the wine business. She was just an overworked secretary with an old tyrant of a boss who took it into his head to send her on ridiculously long errands at a minute's notice.

Itching to be on her way, she made polite conversation about all she had been shown as they walked back through the courtyard. In the hall she thanked Senhor Carvalho for taking the trouble to spare the time. Then he floored her by taking her arm and smiling, "Now I want you to meet my family."

Oh well! What was a few more minutes? Prepared now to be a little late back in Laso, Sarah went calmly enough. They passed the room with the cherry red walls and the curving staircase at the end of the hall. Then through a large airy room filled with sunlight Sarah saw a line of open french windows and beyond, a green lawn bordered by heavy walls and flowering shrubbery.

Laughter and voices filled the air and figures were draped about on the grass beneath a beautiful spreading cedar. Guided through by Senhor Carvalho, Sarah was introduced to at least half a dozen sons, strapping young men who looked as though they had grown up tilling the soil and watching over the grapes, and half as many daughters who obviously had been married off, for toddlers tugged at their skirts or romped over the grass.

Senhora Carvalho, a delicate-looking woman in a high-backed cane chair, rocked a cherubic bundle in her arms while its long-haired mother hung adoringly over them both.

Sarah had smiled and shaken the hand of each member of the family, though she didn't bother to memorise their names. There were far too many, for one thing. And for another it was high time she was on her way. She stood around waiting for Senhor Carvalho to make some offer regarding transport now that all the normal courtesies had been taken care of. But instead he backed off towards the french windows, saying in that charming way of his as he eyed his family, "I'll leave you to get acquainted. You'll stay to lunch, of course."

Sarah's mouth dropped open. But she was given no time to reply. Shooting her a quick smile, the head of the house turned and disappeared with a jaunty step inside. Oh dear, what a nuisance! Sarah tried not to let her frustration show. She didn't want to appear ungrateful, but Portuguese hospitality was something she hadn't taken into account in her tightly planned schedule.

Though she hadn't intended to make any particular effort at being friendly while she waited for the family to eat, a young man of about two years of age was chucklingly attracted by something about her. He tottered around her unsteadily until they both ended up sitting on the grass. In between visions of the noon plane going without her Sarah found herself reluctantly amused by the plump little figure in turquoise romper suit, frilled with lace. His waving, silken dark hair fell over his face as he tumbled about her legs. It was all she could do not to become captivated by his infectious giggle.

The children were taken off by the maids when lunch was announced. Senhora Carvalho went in on the arm of her oldest son, and her husband came out to escort Sarah. The rest followed in chattering ones and twos. The dining-room, with intricately carved walls and ceiling, was a pale saffron colour. Rich red drapes hung at the windows and on the long white-clothed table the plates were patterned in black and gold. Senhor Carvalho took his place at the head of the table. His wife sat facing him at the opposite end. Sarah was shown to a chair about the centre along the side.

The other members of the family settled in around her.

It seemed to her as they waited to be served, that they eyed her with a peculiar interest and something amounting almost to eagerness. She had an odd feeling that the family were gathered together for her benefit, which was ridiculous, of course.

She paid no particular attention to the Portuguese dishes that were brought to the table. The food was good, and that was all that mattered. She would have liked to devote her time solely to getting quickly through the courses. Unfortunately the household seemed to be in a tiresome state of relax and the meal went at a painfully slow pace.

The younger members of the family tossed conversation leisurely up and down the table. Sarah was honoured that they all spoke English for her benefit, but she really had no time for social chat. She had noticed that Senhor Carvalho had laid the deeds which she had brought from England at the side of his plate, and in spite of the chatter everyone's eyes seemed to be constantly drawn towards them.

It was during a silence after a steaming dish of beef and pork had been placed on the table that Senhor Carvalho embraced his family with his gaze and laying his hand lovingly over the documents said with a grateful smile at Sarah, "I think Miss Martindale ought to know that but for her our fortunes might be wavering.'

As Sarah hadn't an inkling of what he was talking about she carried on hurrying through her fish course. She only pricked up her ears when he went on to explain, "For the first time in our lives, Miss Martindale, we find we are having to fight for survival—not here in the grape fields but at the coast where we ship our wine abroad."

The whole table was silent as he continued. "There's talk of building an oil refinery in the district and plans are going ahead to take over Laso harbour, our lifeline to the world. Even as we sit here, a fellow countryman of yours, representing the Pyramid Oil Company, is working to put us out of business."

"The man with the party of surveyors in town?" Sarah lowered her fork momentarily.

"You've seen him?" Senhor Carvalho eyed her sharply.

"He was with his men at the hotel last night," Sarah nodded sourly. "But we didn't meet, thank heaven."

She thought a shadow of relief passed over Senhor Carvalho's face. He began to serve out the next course and the ripple of lively chatter resumed again at the table. As a heaped-up plate was merrily passed along to her the head of the house watched her and said with a twinkling look at her, "You are thinking that we appear only mildly disturbed by this impending disaster?"

As it happened Sarah was doing no such thing. She was wondering how many more courses there were to go and if she was going to manage to get away in time to catch the four o'clock plane from Porto. But for politeness' sake she made an effort to smile in the affirmative.

She noticed the anticipatory glances of the others turn from her and move towards the end of the table, and as soon as he was sure he had her attention Senhor Carvalho tapped the papers beside his plate. "Fortunately for us," he said with a measure of satisfaction, "these documents held by our London partners, and which you have been good enough to bring over, are ancient deeds. They give the Carvalho estate full rights to the harbour and state specifically that if for any reason it is taken over then another harbour must be provided for their use."

"And with our stretch of coastline everyone knows that's impossible," spoke up one of the sons of the family. "There isn't a break in the cliffs for miles."

"Exactly, my dear Adriano." Father and son smiled together.

Seeing that she was the only one proceeding with the business of eating, Sarah pointed out briskly, hoping to bring the subject to a rapid close, "So all you have to do is tell this oil man to take his refinery somewhere else."

The atmosphere had a subtlety which she couldn't

fathom. Everyone eyed her with charitable indulgence. Senhor Carvalho smiled in a dark way and lowering his table napkin from his lips he replied, "In business, Miss Martindale, things are not always as simple as they seem. It's true that no one can deprive us of the use of the harbour, a privilege we have enjoyed for hundreds of years. But Pyramid Oil is a powerful company willing to put up a fight for possession of the harbour. Undoubtedly they would contest the validity of the deeds in court. This would take time, several months perhaps, during which we would lose valuable business."

"And there are those who wouldn't mind seeing us ruined," a younger son put in hotly.

His father twinkled tolerantly down the table. "Perhaps I ought to explain, Miss Martindale." He replenished his wine glass and went on, "By law only grapes from the Douro Valley may be used in the making of port wine. But for centuries the Carvalho family here in the Amorida Valley have been excluded from that rule. And still our wine excels all others. Naturally, as Rodrigues has pointed out, we have rivals."

"Pressure might mount against us." Manoel, the oldest son, put in his piece. "Many would like to see us have to transport our wine harvest as far as Muleira harbour in the north—an impossible task."

"So you see, Miss Martindale," Senhor Carvalho relaxed back in his chair, "we are in no hurry to . . . as you in England might say . . . show our hand."

Sarah laid down her knife and fork and resisting the urge to look at her watch, she asked, "Then how do you intend to get rid of the oil man?"

"For the time being we need to do nothing," Senhor Carvalho's eyes held a sly gleam. "Bryce Taylor, on behalf of Pyramid Oil, will have his work cut out convincing the local population that an oil refinery is a good idea. Besides having to recruit enough local labour, he'll need to buy land and negotiate for road options, and he'll find that the

Portuguese landowner drives a hard bargain." The head of the household smiled as he added, "It may not be necessary to produce the deeds at all."

This brought a chattering response from around the table, after which, much to Sarah's relief, the subject was dropped in favour of other topics. Senhora Carvalho asked her about the current shows in London, and if the skirt was going to be long or short this year, and Sarah spent the rest of the time during the meal trying not to show her ignorance on such matters.

After an agonisingly long period sat rounding off with cups of coffee the family finally broke up. Sarah had never seen so quick a dispersal. Drifting out into the hall with them, Senhora Carvalho asked her if she would like to freshen up and showed her to a quaint washroom under the stairs. When she came out, perfumed with lavender soap, her hat newly positioned on her head, there wasn't a soul to be seen. She looked into the room with the cherry-coloured walls and into another with gilt-framed chairs. The house was ominously silent. Nor was there anyone out in the garden.

Knowing something of continental ways, Sarah wondered if everyone had gone to lie down for the afternoon. A siesta in April! She couldn't imagine it, but the downstairs rooms were certainly deserted. A little crossly she went out to the courtyard and through the gate towards the work-sheds. She would have to find *someone* to drive her back to town. It really was too bad being left high and dry like this. If she had known that the whole place went to sleep after lunch she most certainly would have brought up the matter of transport a lot earlier.

Nothing stirred out of doors. All she could see above the fortress-like walls were the terraces of the vineyards climbing towards a blue sky twittering with birds. She was about to swing away in disgust when she almost collided with Senhor Carvalho standing directly behind her. His expression was one of cheerful imperturbability as though there was nothing at all amiss in everyone disappearing from the face of the earth. He even explained the reason for the deserted work-sheds.

"Today is a public holiday." He waved an arm around the scenery and with the other guided her alongside him. "But tomorrow work will begin once again on the vines. Always there is much to do . . . hoeing, staking, grafting, pruning, and we spray three or four times a year . . . "

His manner was as charming as ever as they walked side by side. But Sarah had had enough of being polite. She stopped abruptly and turning to him in the middle of his conversation she cut in crisply, "Senhor Carvalho, I appreciate your hospitality, but my departure is long overdue. As you rather precipitately dismissed my taxi I need transport to get back to town, and I shall have to ask you to see that I'm driven immediately to the airport at Porto, otherwise I shall miss my plane."

Her host looked at her with those whimsical dark eyes of his. She thought his smile was a little enigmatic as he sighed, "Ah yes, your plane." And bowing her ahead of him, "Shall we go inside?"

Sarah marched smartly in front. She was glad she had spoken up. She didn't want to appear ungrateful, but after all she was a working woman. And only she knew what a state her desk would get into if she stayed away from the office too long.

In the hall she waited for some action. Senhor Carvalho went to a door with a garlanded brass knob and beckoned goodnaturedly. "In here."

It was obviously his own private study. There was a desk, inlaid and patterned with gold, and bookshelves littered with framed family photographs.

Sarah went in only because she saw a phone on the desk. No doubt a chauffeur of sorts could be reached somewhere in the estate. Senhor Carvalho relaxed behind the ornate silver inkstand and taking out a cigarette case he said, smiling, "Do you smoke?"

Feeling ridiculous standing, Sarah had perched on the edge of an available chair opposite. She eyed the rows of cigarettes and replied, sitting glacially erect, "I do not."

Unperturbed, Senhor Carvalho took one for himself and lighting it drew on it leisurely. Sarah, wondering when he was going to get down to the business of ordering a car, listened with a baffled look as he asked her, "How are you liking Portugal?"

"Fine," she lied. Hadn't she done most of the journey giving the minimum of her attention to the scenery?

"I hope," Senhor Carvalho brought his twinkling glance up from the figured ash-tray, "our business conversation at lunch didn't bore you too much?"

"Not at all," Sarah lied again. She was becoming an expert in fencing with polite conversation, a mere preliminary, she was sure, due to some distaste on the part of her Portuguese host for bidding abrupt farewells. And because she felt now she would soon be on her way she added magnanimously, "I hope everything will resolve itself to your satisfaction. I'm sure you'll win your fight with the oil refinery man."

"You're very kind."

For the first time she noticed a trace of strain in Senhor Carvalho's manner. With an uneasy smile he added musingly, "From what I hear Bryce Taylor is an astute worker and brilliant at his job. I have a feeling that as simple farming people we are a poor match for his business skills."

Sarah wasn't sure whether the sly gleam accompanied this last remark or not. There was certainly nothing simple about the sumptuous household; the kind of living the Carvalho family had apparently enjoyed for centuries.

Her host was watching her, and drawing the wrong conclusion from her silence he probed playfully, "But perhaps it's unfair of me to speak ill of a fellow countryman of yours?"

"Please don't worry," Sarah assured him with an icy

glint. "The man's no friend of mine. Thanks to him and his men I had to bed down with the kitchen staff at the hotel last night."

Senhor Carvalho looked thoughtful. "So the surveyors are already in town," he said heavily. "Pyramid Oil are wasting no time."

But we are, Sarah was tempted to say, but refrained. Had the man forgotten that she was waiting for a car? Suppressing a desire to jump up and shout it at him, she fenced on, "Anyway, with the deeds you and your family have little to worry about."

"That's true," her host looked doubtful. "But who can say what means Mr. Taylor will employ to get the things he wants? Or how rapidly he will gain the favour of our rivals in the wine business?"

While trying to remain sympathetic Sarah looked pointedly at her watch. That was the Carvalhos' affair, and she would have to leave them with it. She knew that the head of the family had seen her polite hint. Still he went on drawing leisurely on his cigarette. "What we need," he said, carefully flicking his ash into the silver tray, "is someone on the inside with Pyramid Oil to keep us informed." Then, lifting his dark quixotic gaze, "Someone like yourself, Miss Martindale."

"Me?" Sarah made a pretence of being both flattered and flustered. At the same time she grabbed the opportunity to cut loose from this time-consuming conversation. "I'm fully occupied with the legal paperwork piled on to me by my employer," she prattled, looking again at her watch, "who, I might add, will be wondering what has become of me if I miss that plane."

Senhor Carvalho made no move to hasten her on her way. Instead he said a very peculiar thing. "I think you'll find," he smiled mysteriously, "that Mr. Grapplewick is not expecting you back for some time."

"What? Why that's ridiculous!" Sarah snapped coldly. "I never take my holidays until the back end of the year."

"You misunderstand me, Miss Martindale." Was there a thread of steel blending with the charm in his voice? "I wasn't referring to your stay in the vacational sense, but for the purposes of work."

What *was* the man talking about? While her mind was rapidly struggling to adjust to this strange twist in the conversation he went on, "As you may or may not know, Mr. Grapplewick and I have discussed our problem concerning Pyramid Oil at length. He is well aware of our need to have someone we can trust working with the company to inform us of events, and I agree with him that you are extremely suitable for the job."

"What nonsense!" Sarah scoffed with a smile designed to show the man that she saw through his trickery. "I've been with Mr. Grapplewick for ten years, and as far as my work is concerned," sitting bolt upright, she quivered proudly, "I know he has come to regard me as indispensable. He would never agree to such a proposition."

Senhor Carvalho's smile was disconcertingly self-assured. "We have the phone," he said, reaching a hand towards it without taking his gaze from her. "Do you wish to speak to him?"

"I most certainly do," Sarah replied crisply. The man was bluffing, of course. Because he had business worries he was clutching at any opportunity which offered itself. He would soon learn that her services were not so easily procurable. Also she could let her employer know over the phone the difficulties she was experiencing in trying to obtain transport to leave the house.

While her mind was busy with these thoughts Senhor Carvalho had been leisurely making contact with Southampton over the line. When he heard the voice he was waiting for he handed Sarah the receiver across the desk. Rising, she took it and spoke coolly. "Mr. Grapplewick? Oh, good! I'm still with Senhor Carvalho." She slanted a look of haughty complacency towards the chair. "Unfortunately he's got this odd idea that I've come to help him solve his problems with the oil company . . ."

"That's right, Miss Martindale." All her complaints about the lack of transport died in her throat when she heard her employer's dry chuckle. "I hope you packed enough luggage. I told you to, remember!"

"You're joking, of course," Sarah said tartly, hearing her voice go faint as her limbs went cold.

"Indeed I am not." Her employer's tones changed abruptly. "I have never been more serious. As from today your services have been loaned to the Carvalho family to make use of as they see fit . . ."

"But what about my work . . .? My desk . . .?" Sarah cried with indignation and horror.

"I have a very efficient young woman attending to things at the moment." The voice was smooth. "I think she will cope excellently during the weeks that you are away."

He must have heard her stunned gasp, for he went on testily, obviously anxious to terminate the conversation, "Now don't get difficult, Miss Martindale. The change of scene will do you good. There's a job to be done and I shall expect you to give of your best . . . Goodbye now, and remember . . . our first duty is to our clients."

"But, Mr. Grapplewick . . ." Desperately Sarah tried to cling to the fading tones. "How am I to . . . Wait! Mr. Grapplew . . ." With a click the line went dead and she was left staring disbelievingly into the earpiece. In a daze she dropped the phone back on its hook. Senhor Carvalho, an ironic gleam in his eyes, averted his gaze sympathetically.

Unaware of his existence, Sarah sank into her chair. She was fully occupied battling with various emotions ranging from shocked amazement to icy anger. So they had all known about it all the time! Mr. Grapplewick, Senhor Carvalho and his family. They had planned it between them. Her breath came in short spurts. She'd had a feeling all along that something was not quite right.

And her pride had taken a blow, there was no doubt about that. Mr. Grapplewick had discovered he could manage without her. In fact he had gone so far as to hint that if she refused to do his bidding and went back, she could find herself without a job.

Never to be allowed to sit again at her desk in the offices of Grapplewick, Grapplewick and Small! The thought both terrified and appalled her. It was the only work she had ever known.

A certain amount of throat clearing at the desk reminded her that she was not alone in the room. Senhor Carvalho said with a wicked twinkle, "I trust you have been convinced of your suitability for the job?"

"You mean to spy on this Bryce Taylor and the workings of Pyramid Oil?" Sarah retorted acidly.

"Oh, come now!" The man behind the desk eyed her banteringly. "Spying is such a strong word. Commercial intelligence is the term we use nowadays."

"Whatever the term, the work is the same," Sarah snapped. And with icy calm, "And how am I expected to get the information you need?"

"Naturally we have a plan." Senhor Carvalho's tones hardened. Behind that pleasant exterior was an iron will, one which Sarah could well imagine him wielding to keep his household in order and his strapping sons in their place. With businesslike brevity he continued, "Amongst the local labour he is engaging at this moment, it is common knowledge that Bryce Taylor is looking for a personal assistant to help him with the social side of his job. Tonight you will be installed in your Laso quarters, an embroidery shop of ours of which you will assume ownership. Tomorrow you will apply for the position, pleading boredom at not having enough to do in your shop."

"But how can I expect to get the job?" Sarah expostulated. "I don't speak a word of Portuguese."

Senhor Carvalho smiled. "The people of the wine regions,

Miss Martindale, have always had close ties with England. We speak the language almost as well as you do yourselves, a fact I'm sure Mr. Taylor is well aware of. And from his own point of view I imagine he will prefer an English-speaking assistant."

While Sarah was digesting this she was told, "Once you are established in Laso you will make no contact with us. We will get in touch with you in our own way. Your job will be to report on the progress of Pyramid Oil."

Senhor Carvalho picked up a pen and began to doodle speculatively in between watching her as he spoke. "Bryce Taylor will of course first go for the warehouses and offices and mooring berths at the harbour. Naturally we will hold out against any offer he makes, but that won't deter him. With everything else bought up he will consider he has enough strength to push on. Then he will need land and most certainly road options . . ." A cautious smile played around the lips of the Portuguese winegrower. "It might be that the oil company man will be discouraged earlier in the game. Not everyone will see it his way. Either way our business will continue to run smoothly."

"And if he is successful on every count?" Sarah asked. "If he has everything he needs to build his oil refinery?"

"Then we shall be forced to step in," Senhor Carvalho shrugged, not losing his smile, "and inform him of the harbour deeds."

The situation before her, Sarah considered. What did it matter to her? She had no particular liking for Bryce Taylor. And besides, still stinging from Mr. Grapplewick's indifference, she was filled with a spiteful urge to show him that she could get along equally well without him. It would serve him right if he found out later that he had made a mistake in temporarily dispensing with her services. He would have to struggle along as best he could until her return.

Quivering now, but with malicious satisfaction, she

heard Senhor Carvalho say, "Well, what do you think, Miss Martindale? Are you willing to take on the job?"

Shaken out of her musing, Sarah felt her heart plunge at the question. It was all very well salving her pride by hitting back at Mr. Grapplewick, but how on earth was she going to cope in a job which threatened to be full of intrigue? Her fears and uncertainties made her voice sound high-pitched as she replied, "It seems I have no choice in the matter."

Ignoring her icy manner, Senhor Carvalho rose and said with a pleasant twinkle, "I'm glad you've decided to see it our way." He summoned a maid and when she appeared he turned to Sarah. "And now you would like to rest until this evening? There is a room waiting for you upstairs. If there is anything you need please don't hesitate to ring for it."

The maid beckoned and Sarah stalked out. She followed the dark-clad figure up the curving staircase and along a carpeted balcony overlooking the hall to a door tucked away at the end. Sarah paid no attention to the room. She knew only vaguely that its decor and furnishings were as tasteful as the rest of the house. Her nerves were soaring to a pitch so that once the maid had departed and closed the door she paced up and down unable to believe that this was happening to her.

Nothing had gone right from the start of the trip. First there had been the rush to pack. Thank heavens she had had the foresight to bolt and lock her flat securely. Then there had been the dreary bus journey at this end, and the discomfort of the hotel last night. And now this; forced to work for Senhor Carvalho against an international organisation, and she a mere secretary in a small suburban office.

She wrung her hands, listening to the faraway sounds of the house and wondering how she could have been such a fool not to guess that something was afoot. She was a prisoner here. She paced. No, that was ridiculous. The door was open. She could if she wished walk out of the house. But what then? Her smile curved bitterly. There was nothing for miles in either direction except the Carvalho vineyards.

She sat down, exhausted after the events of the last hour. Senhor Carvalho had stunned her with his proposition. And yet she couldn't dislike the man. He was simply protecting the business interests of himself and his family. How could she blame him for that? And then there was Mr. Grapplewick. Sarah fumed. Nothing would induce her to go running back to him now. Not until he had been taught a lesson. And she could only do that by staying on in Portugal. And in any case, with everything against him around Laso it was quite likely that this oil company man would drop all ideas of building a refinery in a matter of weeks. So what had she to worry about? Nothing.

Just the same, she did worry; so much that she didn't notice the darkness creeping into the room. She rang for nothing, but around nine a tray was brought up to her. She was all for waving it away until it occurred to her that she would be hurting no one but herself by refusing sustenance. Not that she needed much after the magnificent repast at lunchtime.

The maid came to collect the tray at ten and with her departure the house fell into silence. Sarah dozed fully dressed on the bed, with only a small bedside lamp illuminating the room. It was around midnight when she heard a light tap on the door, and struggling up, she went to open it. One of the maids who had served in the dining room at lunch time stood there. Wrapped up against the cold night air, she beckoned with a finger.

Sarah went to collect her handbag, then followed. The hall below was all in darkness save for a small night-light shining down from the chandelier. They went downstairs and out into the night through a side door to where a gleaming black car was running gently on its engine. Sarah saw her suitcase in the back. A bubble of hysterical laughter rose in her throat when she thought of the paltry few possessions she had thrown together for the trip.

Controlling her nervous state, she stepped inside with the help of a darkly-uniformed chauffeur. The other member of the household staff sat beside her and with a muted roar of the engine they pulled discreetly away. In the gloom Sarah recognised the gardens and grounds of the house, after which the headlights picked out the road leading to the opening in the walled enclosure. The tall wrought iron gates were wide open and without slackening speed the car purred out into the night.

The countryside was shrouded in impenetrable blackness. All Sarah saw as they plunged along roads and round bends was the interminable rows of grapevines caught in the gleam of the headlights at the side of the route. The dark-clad shadowy figures in front and beside her, she sat knotted up with tension feeling like a captive in an espionage plot.

They came into Laso far too quickly for her liking. The outskirts with its sprinkling of cottages was clothed in sleep. Further towards the harbour an odd street lamp shone dimly. The car avoided the centre of the town, taking several turns along narrow alleys where the walls of the houses all but brushed the wheels.

They arrived finally in a leafy crescent-shaped space which appeared to be the hub of the town's commercial area. There was a tailor's shop, its showcase lit by a thin strip of fluorescent, and several glass-windowed stores, though most of the businesses were barred and shuttered against the night. From here the car turned off down a side street and pulled up beside a structure standing within a small area of tubbed shrubbery. Its front was painted dove-grey and the two windows, one on either side of the white painted door, were of the curved mullioned kind.

The car doors were opened silently and Sarah was beckoned out. She followed to where a key was pushed furtively into the lock of the white front door. The maid led the way inside. Once he had thrust the suitcase in after them the chauffeur disappeared.

Sarah groped her way along in the dark, aware of thick carpet beneath her feet and the starchy fragrance of new linen in her nostrils. Keeping her ear tuned for the shuffling sounds ahead, she had to fumble her way up a short flight of steps. Once they were round a corner at the top and behind a closed door everything seemed to be all right. The maid switched on the light and threw off her fleecy wrap, smiling as she led the way around the tiny living quarters.

There was a kitchen with flowery wallpaper and modern fittings, and a bathroom and bedroom were tucked away at the end of a small corridor, leading off from the living room, with its round draped table and fringed lampshades. There was no comforting chat to jolly her along. Whether by accident or design it soon became clear that the girl the Carvalhos had chosen to accompany her on this clandestine trip spoke nothing but Portuguese.

Within minutes of arriving the maid was wrapping herself up ready to leave again. Panic seized Sarah and she wanted to beg her to stay. She asked all sorts of inane questions, knowing that nothing of what she said was understood, simply to cling to the girl's presence. But as maid to the Carvalho household the girl clearly had her orders, and with a final smile of encouragement she turned and indicated that it would be necessary for Sarah to come down and lock the door after her.

Together they crept downstairs and through the shop. There was no sign of the black car outside. Having apparently arranged a rendezvous with the chauffeur elsewhere, the maid stole out and disappeared into the night. With banging heart Sarah listened to the muffled footsteps receding. The key of the shop was in her hand. She stared down at it with the horrible realisation. She was on her own.

Trembling, she locked herself in and stumbled around

in the darkness on a new wave of panic. Of course she would never be able to go through with it. She would make a mess of the whole thing. She wasn't cut out for commercial intrigue. At her age she had grown used to pottering along in a dull job with a dull boss. And how she longed now for her desk and the homely routine of Mr. Grapplewick's office!

In her wild groping around she almost fell headlong over her suitcase dumped earlier in the darkness. Calming herself, she gripped the handle and felt her way back upstairs. Inside the pleasantly lit living room she was able to view the situation a little more rationally. She made a tour of all the rooms to try and get adjusted to the idea.

The kitchen cupboard was stocked with food. There was hot and cold water in the bathroom, and fresh towels and sheets in the linen cupboard. She noticed too the English touches cunningly planted around; a calendar of the Lake District on the living room wall and several books on travel, embroidery and cookery on the windowsills.

With sinking heart her lips curled wryly. Senhor Carvalho had thought of everything. Her eye caught sight of a local newspaper opened and folded on the table, and she dropped down on a chair beside it to read the large bold print uppermost. It was an advertisement inserted by the oil company. All their listed labour requirements were printed in both Portuguese and English.

Sarah saw the request for a personal assistant there and the address where the applicants should apply. She was gripped by another bout of wry hysterical amusement when she realised she had come this far without knowing how she was to make contact with the oil boss, then her amusement turned to dread when she thought of what was ahead of her the following day and quickly taking herself off to the bedroom she undressed and slipped wearily between the sheets.

The clamour of activity in the street below woke Sarah the

next morning. For a few moments she was puzzled at her surroundings, then it all came back to her—her meeting with the Carvalhos yesterday and the pose they had arranged for her. Her heart thudding nervously, she rose and slipping on her housecoat made her way to the kitchen. She had no appetite, but she made toast and poached an egg and tried to take an interest in the food.

It occurred to her that she ought to know something about the shop, so later when she had washed and dressed she went downstairs. Though she had no reason to feel pleased with the Carvalho family she had to admire their taste.

The shop was small, but the large bow windows and glass showcases gave a feeling of spaciousness. The fitted carpet was delphinium blue, and a pale blue flowered wall-paper had been used cleverly to pick out nooks and shelves. A prettily designed alcove where customers could browse was furnished with two wrought iron chairs and a table in white, and other wrought iron touches had been used so that the effect was a kind of old-world charm in a modern setting.

Sarah turned her attention to the stock. Being a woman, she found it impossible not to melt at the sight of the exquisite embroidery. The windows were draped with Madeira tablecloths, presumably worked by the island women, and tapestries from the Azores. On the shelves and around the shop there were beautifully textured linen place-mats with matching napkins, monogrammed linen and organdie handkerchiefs, and women's apparel, such as embroidered blouses, linen dresses, and petit-point hand-bags.

Fingering an organdie apron, Sarah ventured a glance outside. The scene beyond the mullioned glass windows was the same as in any small town in England, except that the people passing by had swarthier complexions and the drivers of delivery vans and cars honked their horns long and impatiently.

Urged on to see more, she looked around and spotting a broom behind a curtain in the alcove, opened the shop door bravely and went outside on the pretext of sweeping the front. As she swished away around the tubs of flowering shrubs she saw that there was a carpet shop along the street and a local pottery. How the Carvalhos had paved the way for her to take over the shop she had no idea, but no one appeared curious as she flicked around with a proprietorial air, and her presence caused no stir. Before going inside she noticed the name *Diadema Embroideries* above the mullioned glass windows and saw the wall plate at the end of the street which read *Rua da Trinidade*.

The bell on the shop door tinkled musically. But there was no music in Sarah's heart when she realised she could no longer put off the business of approaching the oil company for a job. Her insides fluttering, she went upstairs. Mercifully she had thrown a change of outfit into her suitcase when packing, so giving the fawn ensemble a rest she dressed in a lavender tweed suit and lavender tweed hat and making sure that the latter was clamped down firmly on to her head picked up her handbag and taking the stairs, went out.

Her hand trembled visibly as she tried to lock the shop door behind her. Schooling herself into appearing nonchalant, she completed the task and dropping the key into her handbag set out at a brisk pace.

The address given in the oil company advertisement was the offices on wharf number three at the harbour. Sarah turned in the direction of the sea with the fervent hope that she would lose herself amongst the narrow alleys and never reach her destination. But much to her disappointment, within a few minutes, she found herself in sight of the green-blue ocean.

The bracing air whipped colour into her pale cheeks, though it did nothing for her quaking insides. She came out on to the harbour front, barely noticing the work-scarred boats bobbing on the waves, and the crescent of sand curving in behind the town. Along the harbour walk her one impulse was to turn and run, but miraculously she kept going searching half-heartedly for the wharf numbers.

A thought struck her as she spotted a large figure three painted on the sea wall up ahead. She wouldn't be the only one applying for the job of personal assistant to the oil boss. Surely even in a town as small as Laso there would be others? And if the job had been advertised for some days it was possible that the position had already been filled.

If she hadn't convinced herself that this was the case nothing would have got her as far as the temporary modern structure, erected on a jutting strip over the water to cope with the oil company's recruiting drive.

Sarah had to pass several officials, men in coloured safety helmets on duty in the area. She was asked to state her business and with plummeting heart was directed to a seat in a glass-windowed partition outside the main office.

She really didn't feel well. Her heart was banging like a big bass drum and her legs felt as though they had turned to water. She could hear a resonant voice behind the frosted glass door in front of her and try as she might she could whip up none of the resentment she had felt for its owner that night at the hotel.

She badly needed something to give her some courage, but all she could do was curse the people who had got her into this mess, and complain fretfully to herself as she clasped and unclasped her handbag that she really wasn't cut out for this sort of thing.

The door in front of her opened suddenly, making her start up in panic. A dark-haired girl came out all smiles and walked off into the sunshine. Sarah relaxed considerably as she watched the figure depart. Obviously the vacancy had been filled. She sat and waited for someone to tell her that there was no point in staying.

All was silent in the office. The waves slapping against

the harbour wall and the cry of seagulls overhead were the only sounds to be heard. Sarah's heart began to thud erratically again. A man came in from outside, making her start up for a second time. Grinning beneath his helmet, he gave her a friendly nod and went into the office.

Sarah's hands gripped her handbag clammily; she toyed with the idea of tiptoeing out and hurrying away. She had almost got as far as rising when the door opened and the man in the helmet told her, smiling as he went out, "The chief will see you now, miss."

Sarah got to her feet, shaking inside. Well, this was it. She couldn't very well run now. Or could she? The door was open and she could see the figure standing behind the desk inside. It was just as she had suspected—he was a different kettle of fish from old Mr. Grapplewick. He looked bigger in the daylight and his square jaw was clamped tight in a line with his mouth as he perused the papers in his hand. She thought he glanced at her rather sharply as she entered the room. This was when she noticed his eyes which were of the palest green.

"Good morning, Miss . . . er . . ."

"Miss Martindale," Sarah replied crisply.

"Take a seat, would you." He strode round her and closed the door.

CHAPTER THREE

SARAH sat down quaking inwardly as Bryce Taylor seated himself behind the desk. Her clothes undoubtedly gave her away, for he stated, eyeing them, "You're English, I take it?"

"I am." Sarah sat up straight and proud.

"And you're applying for the job of personal assistant to me?"

Sarah nodded with ramrod correctness, not allowing herself to forget for one minute that this man had deprived her of a bed at the hotel.

"May I ask what you're doing over here?" The oil boss sat back and viewed her lazily.

"Well . . ." Sarah tried to appear offhand and only succeeded in looking more strained. She gushed forth with her story, hardly daring to pause for breath in case she lost her nerve and dried up. In high-pitched querulous tones she explained how she owned an embroidery shop in town, and all about business being slack. Then, in danger of flagging, she clutched at what she remembered of the hotel manager's conversation. "We don't get many tourists in Laso and . . . I have hardly enough to do. I thought it would be a change to be more . . . fully occupied," she finished lamely.

The oil boss nodded meditatively. He flicked a finger through his papers and asked, "Have you had any experience of this kind of work?"

"Oh yes!" Sarah eyed the littered desks in the room with a practical gleam. She was on home ground now. Without realising it she got somewhat carried away as she prattled, "I can type and I've been used to all kinds of paperwork. I was a secretary for years before I came out to Portugal."

She was so busy mentally tidying up the piles of papers

on the desks, purely from force of habit, that she didn't realise she had talked herself into the job until Bryce Taylor rose and fastening his suit jacket asked, "When can you start?"

Rigid with shock, Sarah got to her feet, "Well, I . . . er . . ."

"This afternoon?" The question was fired at her.

"I . . . I think so." She tried not to look dazed.

"Good! I'll drive you back to your shop and you can arrange to be back here at two."

Sarah was engulfed in panic at his words. "Oh, that really won't be necessary," she said on a strangled note. "I . . . wouldn't want to hold up your work."

"That's okay." He gave her a penetrating look. "I'm through here for the moment, and I've got one or two things to do in town."

Trapped, Sarah went with him to the door and outside past the helmeted men to where his car was waiting. She moved on trembling legs, trying to give the appearance of serenity, while her mind struggled desperately to recall all she had seen of the town. She knew her way back to the shop along the narrow alleys directly inland, the way she had come. But what if the oil man decided to take another route?

Letting in the clutch and zipping along the harbour front, round the crescent of beach and down the hill behind the town, Bryce Taylor said pleasantly, "We usually like to employ someone who has a good knowledge of the vicinity for this job, Miss Martindale. It looks as though you're just what we want."

"Yes," Sarah croaked, watching the only familiar section of sea front disappear before her eyes.

They cruised past rows of fishing cottages and on towards stately old houses, and swinging the wheel casually the oil man asked, still pleasant, "Now, how do we get to this shop of yours?"

Scraping together her composure, and her wits, Sarah

tried to appear brisk and businesslike. "You've come in at the lower end of town," she said crisply. And making a wild guess, "The shopping area is more towards the centre." In a town so small how could she be far wrong?

Obligingly the oil man swung in and merged with the traffic along the narrow streets. Sarah began to feel quite faint. She might have been in the middle of Timbuktu for all she recognised of the balconied houses and occasional shop or café lining the cobbled pavements. She was heartened momentarily when they came out at the strip of ornamental gardens facing the hotel.

Cruising round the little square, the oil man asked cheerfully, "Where to now?"

"I don't run a car," Sarah heard herself saying irritably. "Everything looks different on foot."

She let him twist and wind on through the streets, frantically searching her mind for what to do next. It was the tailor's shop that saved her. She spotted it just as they were curving round towards the crescent of shops and pointing across the space she said triumphantly, "There it is! There's the Rua da Trindade."

"So it is!" Bryce Taylor breathed. He drove through under the trees taking the corner of the Trinidade without a pause, and sure of herself now, Sarah alighted outside the embroidery shop with imperious calm. It crumbled immediately when she saw the oil boss climb out too. He stood back and thrusting his hands into his pockets as he surveyed the front remarked, "A neat little place you've got."

Sarah went to unlock the door. She thought if she made no reply he would go away. But he didn't. He strolled inside after her and browsed around as though he were genuinely interested in ladies' embroidered linens. She tried to look busy beside a glass showcase, opening her handbag and searching for an imaginary item.

At last, when he had been all round the interior, the oil man turned to the door. "Right then," he said briskly.

"I'll see you in my office on wharf three at two o'clock sharp." He went out to his car and slid away into the traffic and Sarah breathed comfortably for the first time that morning.

After the relief she was filled with a feeling of exhilaration. She had done it! She had got herself a job with the oil company! She preferred not to think of the Carvalhos at this moment, or what they expected of her. She found it infinitely more satisfying to see it as a way of playing tit for tat with her old boss who had decided he could get along without her.

She hardly knew what she ate for lunch. Her mind was already focused on the littered desks she had seen earlier, and willingly she presented herself at the oil offices on the stroke of two. Bryce Taylor was up to his eyes vetting suitable applicants for semi-skilled jobs with the oil company along with his employment officer. But he took time off to put Sarah straight on what he expected of her in his office. His orders were blunt and matter-of-fact. "The register of employment." He tossed it at her. "Bring it up to date and classify the new labour . . . professional, administrative, technical, normal," he rapped at her. "And these need tidying up." He showed her the files bulging with letters of appointment, contracts and government stipulations. "That ought to keep you busy for a while."

Sarah felt the panic rising up in her again when she thought of her scant experience. However, once she was left on her own the pure satisfaction of sitting behind a desk again carried her along, and with her appetite for hard work she was soon immersed in the mass of paperwork.

She saw little of the embroidery shop in those first days. She started at the oil offices at nine in the morning and worked late each night in her enthusiasm to put to rights the disorder she found there.

Though the work was vastly different from what she had

been used to in a marine lawyer's office, instead of dealing with paperwork concerning the despatching of an insurance assessor to the Tyneside, she soon learned how to direct twenty tons of concrete to a warehouse wall, and not to a watchman's hut. And in no time she was as familiar with the oil world language of cement, iron rails, tubes and pipes as she had once been with the legal jargon of torts, writs, court orders and prospectuses.

Bryce Taylor was always coming and going. Unless he specifically asked for her assistance Sarah paid no attention to him. She took a pride in her work just as he did in his, and the only outward sign she gave of knowing he was there was in the confident squareness of her shoulders and tilt of her head, at the way she was organising things.

It was almost two weeks before she was reminded of her alliance with the Carvalho family. She arrived at the office one morning to find that someone had dumped a pile of rolled-up literature on the oil boss's desk. Being of a tidy nature she set about filing it all away. It was then she discovered that the rolls were maps.

Purely out of interest at first she spread out one and then another. The personnel map was an aerial view of the countryside and coastline up to about ten miles inland, showing the roads and wharfs, and designed, she assumed, to pinpoint the technicians and where they would be working in the locale. There was a property map, a similar layout except that sections around the harbour were heavily shaded in, and the surrounding land was split up into numbered irregular pieces as though each one represented an owner.

The project map was an artist's impression of what everything should look like when it was finished. Sarah was amazed at the vastness and complex nature of an oil refinery. There were new wharfs, deep-water jetties, submerged pipelines, pumping stations, relay power-stations and lots more that was beyond her. It was the property map that made her think of Senhor Carvalho. This with its wharfside sections of land, some already acquired, was what concerned the wine-grower vitally. Even so she studied it more out of wonder at the fuss men could make over a few bits and pieces of land rather than with the view of passing on the information. If she had been a devious person she would have known to take care to be on her guard while leaning thus over the desk.

As it was she was taken completely by surprise when the door opened and Bryce Taylor strode in. His eye on her and the unrolled maps he said in a brusque and tightly smiling way, "Finding them interesting, Miss Martindale?"

Sarah jumped as though she had been caught trying to steal the Crown Jewels. Because she had absolutely no idea how to carry off an awkward situation, though if she had stopped to think about it she had been doing nothing wrong, she stood there blushing furiously. Luckily the oil boss was emptying his briefcase and leafing busily through the sheaf of papers for those he would require for the day's work. The only remark he tossed at her while the maps burnt a hole under her hands was, "Well, put them up so we can all see them."

Relieved at having something to do, Sarah stumbled and fumbled about. She relaxed, or crumpled was perhaps a better word, only when the oil boss eventually strode off again out of the office leaving her to it.

Limp with nerves as she worked with drawing pins and sellotape, she told herself that she would have to be more careful in the future. If she was going to colour up at every suspicious action she was bound to give herself away in time. Hating the situation she found herself in, she took refuge in her work. Methodically she arranged the maps neatly and securely around the walls of the office. The duplicate sets she filed away.

It was after lunch before she saw Bryce Taylor again. He came in, in his brusque way, eyed the walls approvingly, then gave her her second shock of the day. "Pack all the office gear, Miss Martindale," he told her, "and be ready to move out at a moment's notice."

Move out! Away from her precious desk where she was just beginning to organise everything to her liking? Not again!

Disguising her irritation under a film of ice, Sarah turned from where she was sitting checking through a clip of travel documents and argued coldly, "But I thought we seemed to be progressing satisfactorily under the present arrangements?"

"Our work is just beginning," the oil boss said, smiling energetically. He paced as though to contain the forces driving him on, then swung on Sarah to fire at her, "Have you any idea of the work involved in trying to get an oil refinery launched, Miss Martindale?"

Sarah had, but she had to plead ignorance, didn't she?

The oil boss slapped the project map with its artist's impressions on the wall. "A plant on this scale is an ugly sight," he said harshly. "We've got to convince the local population that it can be done without too much harm to the scenery. We need land, and we need the people's co-operation." He paced again. "We must get acquainted with the aristocracy in the district if we're to get them to give us what we want. The local contractors will have to be wooed, also the town officials." He turned and looked at Sarah with his pale green eyes. "We have to win them all, Miss Martindale."

Having heard all this from Senhor Carvalho, Sarah had been letting her attention wander, watching the determined jaw of the oil man, feeling slightly overwhelmed by his restless vitality. She wasn't in the habit of studying men, so she had no way of knowing his age, but judging from the responsible position he held with the oil company she supposed he must be in his late thirties.

Much to her annoyance she almost jumped when Bryce Taylor fixed her in his pale green sights. Struggling to appear cool, she tried to look attentive as he went on, "What we need now is a place out of town . . . a country house, a villa, somewhere where we can meet the gentry on their own level." He paused to shoot her a glance. "I'm not a married man, Miss Martindale, so you'll have to give me some assistance with the entertaining."

Sarah's heart thumped nervously. Was he suggesting she play the hostess to his possible oil conquests? How could she, knowing what she knew? Besides, the thought of happy gatherings always depressed her. She preferred paperwork to people.

Hoping to throw cold water on the whole thing, she said frostily, "Do you mean to say you're prepared to go out and purchase property simply for the purposes of entertaining?"

"We do things in a big way in the oil business, Miss Martindale," he quirked in his taut way. He glanced at his watch and as though reminded of another appointment added as he turned to go, "I'll pick you up at the shop around ten in the morning and we'll take a look at the houses on the market."

Sarah passed the rest of the afternoon in foul mood. She parcelled up the contents of the filing cabinets and slapped the works ledgers on the desk giving full reign to her irritation. Why was she always being shifted around? Why couldn't anyone leave her to get on with her job in peace?

Later when she was back at the embroidery shop her annoyance turned to apprehension and fright. Bryce Taylor was calling for her in the morning. That in itself was enough to give her the jitters. And on top of this she was expected to help him to choose a house where he could win over the people of the town. The lengths he was prepared to go to get what he wanted shook her considerably. And what if he ever found out that she was working for the Carvalhos?

Making a poor effort at trying to swallow her supper, she was seized with an urge to throw everything into her suitcase and make a run for it. But where would she go? Mr. Grapplewick certainly wouldn't take her back if she opted out at this stage. No. She had burnt her bridges behind her and there was nothing to be done now but to see the wretched thing through.

She slept little that night and rose early to be well prepared for the morning's ordeal. Even so, Bryce Taylor surprised her by turning up at nine instead of ten, the time he had mentioned.

Sarah had been out earlier to buy bread and had left the shop door open. Upstairs her blood froze when she heard the musical tinkling of the bell. Luckily, because of her nervous state she had been ready for ages, and there was nothing to do but tidy around and pick up her bits and pieces.

Moving about the living room, she had expected to go down to bid good morning to the oil boss within a matter of minutes, and it stunned her completely when she heard his footsteps on the stairs. She whipped the last of the breakfast things back into the kitchen and was tremblingly folding the tablecloth trying to give a picture of perfect calm when he appeared.

She made no effort to hide her annoyance at his audacity in invading her private quarters. But he didn't appear to notice. While she busied herself putting things in their place he shrugged with that faint quirk of his, "Don't mind me." And later when she came back from the bedroom she found him fingering over the books on the windowsills and glancing at the objects around the room.

Striving to sound civil, she said, "Well, shall we go?"

The oil boss made no reply. He looked at her and thrust his hands into his pockets. Then he took them out again and began to pace. Obviously he had something on his mind, but Sarah didn't feel inclined to find out what it was. When she wasn't working at her desk she was as uneasy in a man's world as he appeared to be in a woman's.

He took a breath and spoke at last, shattering her last vestige of equilibrium with his words. "I think I explained,

Miss Martindale, that our job is to win the hearts of the local people. If we're going to do that you'll have to . . . er . . . put on some glamour."

Sarah felt the hot colour rising up her throat. She tried not to sway from the effects of it and asked in frosty tones,

"What do you suggest?"

The oil man paced again. He shot a look at her, then rushed on, "Well, that hat. Do you always have to wear it?"

Sarah produced an acid smile over her surprise. She thought she had been doing rather well with her scant wardrobe, wearing the lavender ensemble one day and the fawn one the next. She had found a good dry cleaners and it seemed to her that her outfits were in perfect taste. It came as something of a blow to be told that they were not.

Ignoring the man's impertinence, she marched to the door. She ought to have taken more care going down the stairs. Instead she had to save herself from stumbling once or twice. It was ridiculous to feel hurt at such a small matter, and yet for some silly reason she did.

Downstairs, however, something happened which made the incident seem almost mild in comparison. She had always left the shop round about eight-thirty in the morning, so the problem of customers had never arisen. Today, because of the unlatched door, and the later hour, the hazards of getting outside and locking up the premises unmolested were much greater.

She knew she was in trouble when she saw two head-scarved women conferring together on the pavement over something they saw in the window. If it had been left to her she would have hurried out and so cut off their approach. But Bryce Taylor stood back and said to her, giving them a welcoming bow as they entered, "You'll want to attend to the ladies first."

Sarah gave him a thunderous look. If only he knew that was the last thing she wanted to do! She made an effort to appear businesslike, but the women's gestures and voluble requests completely floored her. "*Eu queira ama lembranca . . . Cici se faz favor . . . Quanto custa este objecto?*"

Hiding her confusion, she tried to guess at what they were waving at and lifted several things out of the window. But this only brought, "*Nao . . . nao,*" and frowns of disapproval mingling with polite smiles.

Sarah was wishing fervently that the floor would open and swallow her up when the oil boss, of whose presence she was only too well aware, stepped forward and reached for a satchet of petit-point handkerchiefs just inside the window. By the cries and nods Sarah was in no doubt that this was what the women had been trying to get her to see.

Calmly he handed her the packet and said, "They want to know how much it is."

Sarah floundered again. Then gathering her wits she took the packet from him and said, peering at it haughtily, "Well, the price will be here somewhere . . ."

Happily it was. The Portuguese women paid and went out, little knowing that they had robbed Sarah of ten years of her life. As she searched out another sachet of handkerchiefs to replace the one in the window Bryce Taylor said testily, "I manage better when the shop isn't so I would have thought you'd have picked up a bit of the language?"

Sarah eyed his big frame and gathering up her handbag said testily, "I manage better when the shop isn't so crowded."

As they went out to the car she wondered if her shortcomings as a linguist would lose her her job. But though the oil boss was thoughtful he made no further comment on the matter.

He drove to the outskirts of Laso and they spent the time going over the various properties that were up for sale. The outing wasn't a success. Every house they looked at was either too small for entertaining purposes or too far out of town to be practical.

It was almost dark when they arrived back at the shop. It had been a bad day and Sarah climbed out of the car glad to be back. She locked up as Bryce Taylor drove away and went upstairs to prepare herself a meal before retiring to bed for an early night.

The next morning, to safeguard against the disasters of the previous day, she put a closed sign *Encerrado* on the shop door after returning with fresh bread. And to discourage anyone who might be tempted to come and try the door and find it open she lowered the blinds inside the display windows. The thought of another day of house-hunting depressed her. But it was obvious that Bryce Taylor would go on looking until he found what he wanted. And as his personal assistant she was expected to know something about these things.

The day was warm and sunny. She ate her breakfast pondering on the shafts of gold streaming in through the living room window. Later she went downstairs and searched amongst the embroidered garments hanging on the rails. There was a blouse with long sleeves and a button-up neck, embroidered palely down the front in a not too flamboyant design. She took this back upstairs with her. It was a good fit and went passably with her fawn skirt.

Her hair caused her some considerable irritation. She always wore it short, and without a hat she had no idea what to do with it. It was pale like the colour of buttermilk and totally unsatisfactory. She ended up by making a kind of feathery fringe around her face and arranging it in a similar way round to the nape of her neck.

She picked up her handbag and moving about the living room, tried to feel nonchalant about her appearance. But when the shop door bell rang below and a footstep sounded on the stairs she stood rooted with agonised indecision. What on earth had possessed her to think she could wear anything but her normal garb? Her hands flew about her blouse and face. What must she look like? And her hat! How could she go out without a hat?

She was seized with a desire to run to the bedroom and quickly don the things she felt at ease in. But there was no time. Bryce Taylor was already entering the room, and rather than let him see her dilemma she peered and fumbled shakily for the usual imaginary object in her handbag.

Flicking her glance upwards, she pretended not to notice his look of mild surprise. She fumbled madly as he inclined his head and gazed at her critically. And when, after what seemed an age, he mused drily, "Well, it's an improvement anyway," Sarah cursed herself for blushing like a schoolgirl.

As they went downstairs and out to the car, the oil boss told her that they would be exploring the eastern outskirts of the town where the properties which were known to be more exclusive would possibly prove more suitable for the oil company's requirements. Sarah certainly hoped so. She didn't care for riding round in a car all day. She longed to be back behind her desk where she could keep a proper control over her emotions.

CHAPTER FOUR

THE outlook didn't seem too promising at the start. Out where the country was wooded the properties on the market were fewer and much more difficult to locate, and the ones they did find had to be seen to be believed. There was a miniature castle with high-vaulted ceilings and wide stone archways, as cold and cheerless as an armoury museum, and a newly built air-conditioned structure with glass walls and rooms panelled in mauve and gold.

Sarah wasn't remotely interested in houses anyway and by late afternoon, after covering the entire eastern fringes of the town and having to make do with an insipid lunch at a roadside *pousada*, she wanted only to get back to town. Bryce Taylor's tenacity annoyed her. She would have thought they had seen enough monstrosities for one day. But no, he had to turn off down yet another side lane and with set features she sat stiffly upright while they traversed a narrow valley and then started to climb.

She had long since shut her mind to her surroundings, so she noticed nothing on this particular trek until they were stepping out of the car beside a small patio garden inside green iron gates. She had told herself she wouldn't put herself out at all by looking at the view. This left her totally unprepared for the effect of leafy clouds of yellow-dappled eucalyptus trees sloping down to the blue-green ocean less than a mile away.

To combat the shock of—was it pleasure? which threatened to root her to the spot, she quickly reminded herself of the chore to be got through of viewing the property. As Bryce went to put the key in the front door she started on her round of the exterior.

The grounds were fairly extensive. There were mimosas and graceful pepper trees and a loggia of trailing vines at the side that looked out on to flowering fruit trees. At the back there was a sweep of garden and lawns and at the far side a leafy courtyard sheltered luxuriant semi-tropical vegetation.

Drifting under some kind of spell, Sarah went through the courtyard and into the house. She had never in her life before been on a house-hunting expedition, yet somehow she knew exactly what this one would look like. The chestnut-panelled walls, slanted beamed ceilings and leaded glass windows were just what she expected.

The huge main room had a large walk-in fireplace and this, along with most of the others, had window-seat nooks. The dining room overlooked a hillside of villas and orchards, and upstairs one had a view of the leafy courtyard below or the green stretches of lawns and gardens.

Sarah noticed that the window façade in every case allowed the sun to pour through, making for well-lit and cheerful rooms, twelve in all. The main lounge with its views of the sea, she could guess, would be brilliant with sunrises and sunsets. The whole house, though empty and bare, was warmed by honey-toned parquet flooring.

Sarah felt she must take another stroll outside. She was looking down past the eucalyptus trees when the oil boss's footsteps, which she had heard clicking all over the house, came down the main staircase and outside. As he strode towards her she felt the wash of his enthusiasm. "What do you think, Miss Martindale?"

Though she permitted herself just a brief glance his way she was struck by the buoyancy of his step; the light of pleasure which seemed to darken the green eyes. Did hers look like that? Trying to play down her own enraptured impressions of the house, she said in her staid fashion, "In my opinion it's the best we've seen so far."

"Good." He seemed satisfied with her reply. His usual inflexible jaw relaxing slightly, he looked at his watch. "Let's see, today's Wednesday. I'll clinch the sale tomorrow. Friday I'll pick you up and we'll take a run down to Lisbon."

"Lisbon?" Sarah eyed him coldly. "Whatever for?"

"The place needs furnishing," Bryce shrugged. "Only the big stores will know how to handle it. We'll probably have to make a week-end of it, so you'd better take tomorrow off."

Sarah got back into the car with the feeling of caged butterflies in her stomach. No one told her she would have to spend so much time tearing about the country. And always with Bryce Taylor. When was she going to be allowed to get back to the sanctuary of her desk?

That night at the shop she sat around uneasily, and the next day she tried to take her mind off things by wandering around down by the harbour. She wasn't in the habit of noticing the views, but she supposed with so many car jaunts she must be growing used to the idea. Anyway, the rolling white breakers down on the beach caught her eye, and she was more than a little fascinated by the high-powered brightly-painted boats the fishermen used. The wind lifted her hair which she had quite forgotten used to be imprisoned inside a hat, and the salt spray stung her cheeks, giving them a most unusual rosy bloom.

She stepped amidst the ropes drying on the beach and mingled with the Laso women in sombre black shawls who were slitting and gutting fish and tossing them into shallow baskets. Children kicked up the sand on her clothes. She ought to have been cross, but there was a sparkle in the air that kept her moving with a light step.

Up on the quay she permitted herself a brief glimpse along towards the warehouses and wharves to the right of the beach and across to the wild open stretches of country on the opposite side of the crescent of sand, where the map had shown the artist's impression of the oil refinery. Apart from this she made every effort to forget the nerve-racking situation she found herself in.

Of course it all came back to her when she returned to the shop. She ate her supper worrying about the distance by road to Lisbon—over three hundred kilometres, according to the map. She would never do it! A four- or five-hour drive in the car beside Bryce Taylor! How on earth would she pass the time? With palpitating heart, her hands fluttering nervously, she picked out the thickest book she could find amongst the works on the windowsills, and to this she added half a dozen periodicals from the magazine rack. Placing these next to her handbag, she went to bed slightly easier of mind.

She rose far too early the next morning, then wasted the time keeping her ears tuned apprehensively instead of getting on with the jobs that needed doing. She possessed no week-end case, so she had to improvise with one of the embroidered bags from the shop. She donned her lavender tweed suit, freshly cleaned and pressed. It was the only thing for the city. And her hair—she was sure it looked much too frivolous for a business trip. Softened now with the wind and the sun, it gleamed paler than ever. Working at it, she found that if she parted it in the middle and smoothed it low over her brow and ear on either side, she had almost enough to catch it in a tiny roll at the back of her head. Yes, she liked that. It was much more *her*.

She didn't wait upstairs for Bryce Taylor, but kept a lookout from behind the lace curtains for his car. As soon as she saw it drawing up she got herself downstairs into the shop. When he opened the door Sarah was there holding her bags and books ready to go.

After the briefest of "Good morning's" she carried everything out herself to the car. But she had to have the door opened for her before she could manoeuvre herself in beside the driving seat. She only remembered, after congratulating herself on making an unfussy start to the day, that she had forgotten to lock the shop door. Of course, then she had to struggle out again and hurry to perform the task and this made her twice as flustered.

The oil boss obviously didn't want to waste any time and as soon as she was settled he started off and drove through the town. It wasn't long before they were leaving the outskirts of Laso behind them.

The road was straight and smooth. The car, being of the finest make, purred effortlessly along. Sarah began to wish it would rattle and bang about a bit. It was far too quiet inside the car for her peace of mind. At least she had her magazines and book, and after Porto she took up the latter and put on a studious air.

It could have been that Bryce Taylor too found the silence a little overpowering inside the car, for after a while he switched on the radio. Sarah battled with her irritation while he listened to the news and several talks in Portuguese. It was all right for him, knowing something of the language, but how did he expect her to read with that noise going on? Later, the music he chose was just as annoying. It wasn't the quality of the orchestras he picked but the volume he turned it up to which made it impossible for her to soak up the printed word.

They stopped for lunch at Coimbra and worked throughout the meal making a list of the various rooms to be furnished in the newly purchased house, and deciding on the staff that would be needed to run it. Sarah wouldn't have had it any different. She knew of no better way to pass the time than to immerse oneself in hard work of some kind.

The sun blazed in through the car windows during the afternoon. As they sped south, Sarah found she had to remove her thick tweed jacket or melt in the heat. She folded it methodically with the lining outside and laid it neatly across her knee. Then she took up her book again. Though she had been carefully turning the pages since the journey had begun she couldn't have told anyone what the story was about. Bryce Taylor kept the radio blaring. When one music programme finished he turned to another. And that was how they arrived in Lisbon, just as dusk was shrouding the city.

"Too late to do anything now," said Bryce, weaving

through the traffic. "We'll go straight to the hotel."

Watching shoppers eddying past glittering store windows, Sarah was bound to admit she was too spent by the trip to think of joining them. She was a little startled at the prestigous appearance of their accommodation. The Sheraton Hotel, on a prominent boulevard overlooking a green park, she was sure must be the tallest building in Portugal. And once the car was parked and she was inside the brilliantly lit building, it was more than plain that the clientèle was chock full of diplomats, business tycoons and film stars.

Slightly dazed at the magnificence, she stood in her tweeds clasping her bags and books to her while Bryce Taylor arranged things at the desk. He came back to her through the motley gathering in the foyer and waved her ahead with him. They followed a page to a battery of lifts and as they ascended he told her, "We're on the fourth floor. Rooms four-o-eight and four-o-nine. I've ordered the meals to be sent up."

Sarah gave a businesslike nod of approval.

The page opened the doors of the rooms when they arrived and left them with the keys. Sarah disappeared quickly inside hers and closed the door briskly behind her. Dropping her things, she strolled critically around the spacious air-conditioned bedroom and into the adjoining all-marble bathroom. She knew the oil company was paying for all this, but all she could think was, what a shocking waste of money. French windows opened on to a small balcony.

Outside below was the gentle roar of traffic, and across on a hillside, tall houses and buildings spangled with lights were painted with the violet glow of dusk. Sarah was letting her gaze wander still further upwards to where a golden-lit castle shone above illuminated greenery when a sound nearby made her tense. Beyond the wrought ironwork screen separating them Sarah knew the oil man had come out on to his balcony. Silently she shrank back inside.

She left the windows open because the air was warm, but she preferred to take what she could of the outdoors after that perched at the end of the bed. Her evening meal came to her on a gleaming trolley. She had to admit that the food was superbly cooked and served, but she still thought they could have managed just as well in a less expensive establishment.

Later, wrapped in her housecoat, she ventured out on to the balcony again. There were chairs out there and a table. Sarah would have liked to sit taking the air and watching the city by night, but what stopped her was the blurred shape beyond the screen. Curses! Bryce Taylor was sitting out there. And what was more, it smelled as though he was puffing at a pipe. She had never seen him with one. But of course he wouldn't smoke it when he was working, would he?

She hung about in the doorway of her room. It wasn't that his pipe smoke bothered her. If anything she found it rather fragrant. But how could she sit out there knowing he was doing exactly the same thing at his side of the screen? She just couldn't.

Arms folded, she waited in the shadows of her room hoping he would go in after a while. But he sat and sat and puffed at his pipe until the traffic dwindled down below and the streets became deserted. He was still sitting there when Sarah took herself off irritably to bed.

She was awakened early the next morning by the arrival of her breakfast trolley. It was really quite a beautiful day. She had no idea that a sky could look so blue or that a city with all its crowded buildings and roof-tops could look so enchanting. She had never before had breakfast out in the open, but for once she was going to try it.

She hurried to shower and to wrap herself in her housecoat, then carefully she pushed the trolley of gleaming silverware over towards the open windows. She didn't get as far as pushing it outside. One look and she recoiled hastily back into her room. Bryce Taylor was already out there, hogging his terrace as usual. Sarah could hear the clink of his tea cup, the rattle of his morning paper. Crossly she wheeled the trolley towards the indoor table and breakfasted, making do with what she could glean of the view from there.

Afterwards she wasted no time in getting dressed and grooming herself ready for the outdoors. To Sarah it was unthinkable not to be prepared for the day's work. When Bryce Taylor rang her door bell she was waiting on the other side of it with her handbag tucked under her arm. He gave her a cheerful good morning, oblivious of her spiteful look. After all, *he* had enjoyed his terrace to the full, hadn't he!

He told her on the way to the lift, "We've got a heavy day ahead of us, Miss Martindale. We'd better get straight down to business."

Sarah nodded and stepped along briskly. She was fully in agreement with that. Downstairs they crossed the busy foyer and went out to the car. The traffic was as furious as ever. Sarah noticed that the oil boss remained cool despite the frantic honking of horns and the excitable meanderings of the Portuguese motorists.

Weaving amongst white buildings, they came out eventually at the sloping end of the green park which was visible from the hotel. Sarah wasn't one for sightseeing, but she turned a casual glance back at the statue atop a tall white plinth which looked down over the city and the sea below. Past palm trees, azaleas and rhododendron bushes the car descended the sloping, impressive Avenida da Liberdade to Lisbon's shopping centre.

"I'm not sure which of these will prove most useful." Bryce Taylor waved a sheaf of advertising brochures he had gleaned from somewhere as they parked the car. "We'll just start with the biggest store and hope for the best."

He led the way along a mosaic sidewalk and into an imposing entrance. Sarah was dazzled by the interior displays but not impressed. Purple carpets, glittering chandeliers and glass and chromium-plated coffee tables somehow left her unmoved. Tall swivel-mirrors, cut-glass globes and transparent inflated plastic armchairs didn't do anything for her either. Beside Bryce Taylor she toured each floor and with him she came down and out to the street again.

She followed him into another store which had an exclusive air about it and wandered through showroom after showroom bright with aristocratic glamour. Though everything was a blaze of colour, emerald green, bright orange and peacock blue upholstery, nothing caught her eye particularly.

They toured the main shopping area on foot. Sarah had never seen so much interior elegance and glitter. She was beginning to think that all Lisbon homes must be extravagantly streamlined and boringly conventional, when they came upon a tall narrow store in a side street with a few bits and pieces in the window. She felt warmed immediately by the flawless old world aura they encountered in the store.

Instantly her eye was taken by an antique refectory table. Before she could get to it Bryce was ahead of her. He smoothed his hand lovingly over the mellowed surface and mused, "This would be great for the hall."

Sarah couldn't resist touching it too, though she replied in her staid businesslike tones, "I couldn't agree more." They looked around and Bryce pointed with boyish enthusiasm. "How about using old wooden chests as coffee tables?"

Sarah nodded, unable to keep the inspired light out of her eyes. "I was thinking the same."

"And Chippendale-style chairs, I think, don't you?" He strolled on.

"Perfect," Sarah breathed, a little dazed at her forwardness. What did *she* know about furnishing a house? Her own flat, fitted out by her military-styled father, was utilitarian and rather cold in concept. Yet somehow she knew that all this was right for the house on the hill at Laso. Bryce Taylor obviously felt it too. It was strange how his inner excitement seemed to be in accord with her own.

Together they wallowed in the atmosphere of hammered-copper trestle tables, and wrought iron wall sconces, each going for the same object at the same time. It wasn't long before Sarah's notebook was filled with the scribbled lists of their purchases. They bought autumnal-toned sofas and armchairs; burnt orange mushroom lamps, fine Italian and Portuguese wood pieces, oriental rugs for the floors, and much, much more.

Sarah's cheeks were in danger of becoming a little flushed when Bryce said, looking equally exhilarated, "How about some lunch? We can do the rest this afternoon."

"Very well," Sarah said, averting her gaze and reminding herself quickly of her station.

They left the assistants arranging package and transport and went back to the car. Sarah had no idea where they were going to find a meal amidst the rush and push of the city, but Bryce appeared to have something in mind. He drove through the honking traffic until they came into an area of narrow streets. Then leaving the car in a secluded alley he led the way to an amber-lit doorway.

Sarah followed him into what seemed to be a tuckaway refuge for successful businessmen. She felt ridiculously shy in the tavern-like atmosphere, in an interior decorated with everything from violins to zithers; from stirrups to iron plaques. But Bryce, perfectly at ease, escorted her through to one of the alcove tables.

Tiny dishes of caviar, liver patè and cream cheese were placed before them. On the menu there were such things as Spanish-style clams, pepper steak, roast kid and even frankfurters with sauerkraut, and desserts, like rum crêpes. The alcove tables were far too intimate to Sarah's way of thinking. She felt a trifle suffocated sitting across from the oil man, cut off as they were from the rest of the room.

However, there was no denying that the food was appetising and with the list of the morning's purchases to be checked through, and the further buying of window drapes and wall decor for the house to be considered—a subject which Bryce discussed as enthusiastically as she did herself—Sarah found the meal surprisingly enjoyable.

It was after three when they emerged from the rosy amber-lit interior of the restaurant into the fading sunshine. They had to get back to the shops quickly as there was still much to do. The curtain material took the longest to run to earth. Sarah was of the opinion that solid printed fabrics were best for the windows of the house, and Bryce collaborated with her on this. But nothing of what they had in mind turned up until late afternoon when they came upon a store with an abundant supply of what they had been looking for.

After that it was fairly easy going. Browsing amongst shops displaying Mozambique and Macao handicrafts, they bought contemporary hand-woven tapestries, rare prints and several pieces of Portuguese china for the wall niches of the house.

The shops were closing their doors when they finally made their way back to the car. It was only then that Sarah realised she was exhausted. She was surprised, too, to discover how the time had flown. It was almost eight o'clock and the sky had the lavender tint of evening when they arrived back at the Sheraton Hotel.

They went through the foyer with its atmosphere of minks and poodles to the lifts. Upstairs outside their doors Bryce said a little brusquely, as though he wasn't used to making conversation other than that which concerned business, "The hotel's got a rooftop restaurant. We might as well put the firm's money to good use and dine there tonight."

"Very well." Sarah wasn't in the habit of talking about

anything but work either and that was the best she could do. "At what time?" she asked in the tones she used for jotting down appointments in her notebook.

"Oh, around nine-thirty." The oil boss slackened his tie and Sarah nodded and went into her room.

She stripped and with her housecoat tied around her sank on to the bed. She thought she might doze for a while after the rigours of the day, but her mind was restless with thoughts of the evening to come and it was amazing how fast the fatigue fell away from her.

She forced herself to lie still for an hour, then rose and took a hot shower. Bryce Taylor rang her bell at nine-thirty. As promptly as if she had been answering his request to type out a letter Sarah went to join him.

CHAPTER FIVE

THEY took the lift up to the very top to where the rooftop restaurant crowned the tower of the building.

Sarah was quite startled by the shimmering sky views of Lisbon by night. If she hadn't been her usual composed self it might have taken her breath away. While she walked with Bryce across the outdoor terrace her eyes lingered on the river and bridges strung with lights.

Adjoining the cocktail lounge, the restaurant was a glassed-in interior where no view of the rainbow neon-lit city escaped the eye. To Sarah's mind it was all very grand. They were led across opera red carpeting past tables winking with silver and cut glass. Muted lamps enhanced the view. Beyond the tables one had an impression of elegant touches of gilt and tasteful flower arrangements.

The restaurant was already three-quarters full, but Bryce must have made a reservation, Sarah supposed, for they were guided without question to a table near the windows. She was thankful in a way for the dark expanse of sky and blazing panorama below, to one side of their table. It alleviated the sense of strain she felt dining in such a setting with the oil boss.

She wished, in a way, she could take it as he was doing. He appeared reasonably relaxed and went through the menu with her quite as though they were checking over a business pamphlet together. She had to confess that she had no idea what *espadon fume* was. He seemed to enjoy introducing her to razor-thin sliced smoked swordfish served with half a lemon wrapped in white gauze to prevent seeds from falling on the fish. She was bound to admit to him that its delicacy was memorable.

He consulted her about wines, but in the same way as the food, she left it to him. She felt it only right to compliment him on his choice when after all each glass blended perfectly with the course in question. Of course, she wasn't in the habit of drinking wine. She felt the faint flush of pink on her cheeks. She noticed too that Bryce's rugged features were occasionally transformed by the suggestion of a sloping smile. She considered it clever thinking on his part to have ordered a souffl for two, which was just about ready for dessert time.

The restaurant was now a-buzz with conversation around the tables where the hotel guests were making the most of the cuisine and the flawless service. Waiters glided back and forth, and friends met and chatted in the golden pools of light, though Sarah couldn't say she noticed much of it. Her gaze was directed more towards the dark outside and the bejewelled city spread below them. And she knew Bryce's Taylor's attention was aimed mainly that way. He pointed out to her at one time the three hundred and fifty-foot stone statue across the river Tagus, illuminated against the skyline.

They were drinking coffee which, as Sarah was told, came from Timor. With the purple skyline before her, she had quite forgotten where she was until a voice, all feminine surprise, jerked her back to reality. "Bryce! Bryce Taylor! What are you doing over here?"

The oil boss must have already turned, for when Sarah looked he was on his feet, towering beside a ravishing creature the like of which Sarah had seen only in the news-reels of film premieres and theatre first nights. The woman's slender figure was encased in a pure gold sequinned dress up to her ample bosom which was daringly supported by one slender gold strap around her neck. Matching golden arm gloves finishing on a line with the curving dip of her dress did everything to enhance the bare expanse of shoulders. She wore huge emerald drop earrings framed in gold and a golden rose was pinned in her burnished copper hair. One viewed the flawless make-up and the full red lips through the most flattering of golden veils.

While Sarah's bedazzled gaze was taking all this in Bryce's face had collapsed into a boyish grin and he was saying in a deep lazy voice which Sarah had certainly never heard before, "Hello, Maggie. We're trying to get an oil refinery launched outside Porto." He turned back to the table as though he had just remembered he wasn't alone and added, "This is my personal assistant, Miss Martindale."

"Hello."

Sarah had her hand clasped, over-warmly she thought, in the silken white grip. "How do you do," she replied a little stiffly, feeling acutely conscious of her tweed suit and neatly parted hair drawn back over her ears.

The waiter chivalrously came along with a chair and leaning over the table lamp voluptuously, Maggie joined them.

"Miss la Fay is an entertainer," Bryce informed Sarah, giving his sloping smile to the golden vision sitting next to him.

As though she thought it was too polite a word Maggie threw up her hands and laughed throatily. "I'm a singer of sorts. I've just done a tour of the States and a couple of spots in South America which almost killed me. I'm booked for a week in Lisbon, then I'm off to Italy to languish in the sun for a while." She slipped an arm through that of the oil boss and twinkled at him accusingly. "And what's new in the oil world? Do you realise it's three years since I've seen you." To the murmured reply, "Is it as long as that?" she eyed him with a wicked gleam and giggled, "Do you remember that night in Cairo when you threw Toby Wheeler into the swimming pool?"

Sarah was on her feet. She said with a smile of sorts as she picked up her handbag, "If you don't mind, I think I'll go to my room now."

"Of course Miss Martindale." Suavely Bryce Taylor rose to his feet. He mentioned as an afterthought as she passed by his chair, "And . . . er . . . as it's Sunday tomorrow you'd better take the day off."

"Thank you. Goodnight, Miss la Fay." Sarah walked quickly out of the restaurant. As she crossed the outdoor terrace she didn't look at the view. The day had somehow turned stale on her. She went down in the lift smiling sourly at Bryce's magnanimous gesture. Had he forgotten he had already given her one day off this week?

Moodily in her sumptuous bedroom she prepared for bed. She ought to have been ready to sleep the clock round after the hectic day of shopping, and it annoyed her to find that she was very wide awake. After half an hour or so spent trying to doze she tied her housecoat around her, and drifting out on to the balcony sat down in one of the chairs. The view, though more restricted at this level, was just as pretty, Sarah was ready to admit that. But she was mainly concerned with the empty feel of the balcony next door. Bryce wasn't back yet. She tried not to notice the way the breeze accentuated the silence. It was strange. It had irritated her when he had never left his chair on his own balcony. Now when she had the whole view to herself she felt just as ruffled.

More than once she slid a glance at her watch as she sat rigidly enjoying the sea-scented air. At midnight the breeze turned chilly and she had to go in. She closed the glass doors behind her with a slight clatter. In bed she lay with one ear off the pillow. Not that she was remotely interested in listening for the sound of Bryce Taylor's door. It was simply that she couldn't get to sleep. At one o'clock she heard a bell chime faintly somewhere in the city, and after that she remembered no more.

Because it was Sunday her breakfast trolley arrived an hour later the following morning. Sarah didn't mind. She had no idea how she was going to fill the day. She had little experience of foreign cities, but it was obvious she couldn't sit in her bedroom all day.

She ate without opening her glass doors. She had no wish to see the view this morning. After breakfast she washed and dressed and went out. Turning the key in the lock of her door, then dropping it into her handbag, she had time to cast a casual glance towards Bryce's room. All was silent there.

She took the lift down and passed fur-stoled women and men in black homburgs in the foyer. Outside in the sunshine she was considerably nervous of the traffic. Though it was Sunday there seemed to be more cars than ever thundering along the wide boulevard. Feeling quite unsafe, she made a dash with the rest of the pedestrians who flocked with noisy bravado in the path of the lethal machines.

Everyone on foot seemed to be making for the green park not far from the hotel. Sarah decided that it was as good a place as any to start with. She was more than a little impressed by the scene when she arrived.

On the slope of a hill manicured green lawns flowed inwards on either side to meet a brilliant stream of red flowers. And coursing down the centre between the twin flower borders was a tremendous stretch of green geometry in the form of foot-high cleverly clipped hedges. Boys and youths kicked footballs here on the greener than green grass, using the square enclosures of the hedges as miniature football fields. In other sections, young mothers and grandmothers beamed over toddlers just learning to walk. And there down at the lower end of the park was the statue and square that they had passed yesterday in the car. Sarah recognised the rather autocratic figure at the top of his ornate pedestal. And what a tremendous eye view he had looking out over the white panorama of the city and the blue sweep of bay.

After studying the vista herself she walked down the sloping paths, mingling with the Sunday strollers. In the palm-tree-lined square she derived a certain satisfaction from glancing at the base of the white carved plinth in passing. The name *Marques de Pombal* told her nothing except that he must have been an important man in his day to occupy such a favoured position in the city.

Crossing the circular space, she set off briskly down the tree-lined Avenida da Liberdade. She soon learned that it was much longer on foot than it had seemed in the car. But telling herself she was out for the day, she stepped along stoically. In a way it was pleasant marching past flower gardens and ponds with swans. Later there were outdoor cafés, airline offices, restaurants and shops.

Her feet were beginning to ache, and Sarah would have liked to stop for a drink, but she couldn't see herself sitting at one of the pavement tables surrounded by groups of animated Portuguese. Even as she walked by, the men followed her with their glances of amused pity because she was on her own. No. Though the sun was hot and her throat was becoming parched with dust, she would most certainly keep going.

In downtown Lisbon all the shops were closed. Sarah kept on until she came to another square, bordering the river Tagus she supposed it was, though she always thought of that great expanse of rippling blue water as the sea. There was a striking equestrian statue here. To Sarah's critical gaze the square had beauty and harmony, though being one of those who didn't hold with cars monopolising one's whole existence she deplored its present use as a parking lot.

She hadn't really intended to come this far, but reluctant to turn back to the hotel just yet, she decided somewhat recklessly to explore a little further. She soon knew she had made a mistake when turning east along the waterfront she found herself wandering through twisting narrow streets. She had no idea that she was in the ancient Moorish district of Lisbon, but something about the mediaeval houses, the winding alleys, some no more than stairways, made her feel a little uneasy. Of course the simple way would have been to turn back in the direction of the square, only she wasn't quite sure which way that was now.

Briskly she kept going, refusing to believe that there was anything to worry about. Hadn't she always been used to faring alone? It was ridiculous to feel uncertain in these strange surroundings simply because Bryce Taylor wasn't here to guide her.

Climbing one and then another of the sloping cobbled streets, she forced herself to notice the flower-draped balconies and old wall lanterns, even though plump dark-haired women, gossiping and exchanging small talk from the windows of the tall tenements, stared at her in an unbearably curious manner. In a tiny square she came upon barefoot children and fishwives selling the latest catch from the sea. And in another space housewives armed with bottles and jugs, were arguing volubly, and crowding around a public faucet. Luckily the men were too busy trying to decide whose turn it was next to draw water to notice Sarah as she hurried by.

The narrow labyrinthine streets seemed unending, and Sarah's feet were aching abominably. She was sure she must have walked miles. She was horrified, when she looked at her watch, to see that it was after three. Obviously she would have to eat soon if she was to avoid collapsing in a heap on the cobbles. She had passed several dubious-looking establishments tucked away in the alleys, taking care each time to avert her gaze as she did so. But when a smoke-filled doorway appeared at the top of a gruelling flight of steps, she knew she could go no further.

The place was filled with craggy-faced, black-bereted men with stained-toothed smiles and work-gnarled hands with which they gesticulated wildly. The noise was shattering and but for her trembling legs Sarah doubted whether she would have had the courage to enter. However, once inside she put on a bustling show of knowing exactly what she was doing, and this carried her into the cavelike recesses past strings of peppers and garlic and hanging hams and sausages. There was a serving counter laden with ceramic bowls, wine bottles and crocks of food, none of which, Sarah thought, looked in the least bit appetising.

It could have been that the proprietor, an elfin figure in a large apron, had entertained the occasional tourist in his café, for he didn't stare at Sarah as though she had two heads, as everyone else had done. Instead he gave her a bow and beckoned her eagerly forward, and thankfully Sarah hid herself at one of the cubbyhole tables. She explained that she would like something to eat and drink, and the diminutive Portuguese must have known what she meant, for with a smile and a flourish he disappeared.

He brought her a large bottle of purified water, then quickly vanished again. Blissfully Sarah quenched her thirst and surreptitiously eased her feet around in her shoes. Nothing else happened for half an hour or so, and she was wondering anxiously if the bottled water was all she was going to get. Then the food appeared. She had rather hoped, after sitting so long, that the meal would prove worth the interminable wait, but her heart sank when she gazed at the golden-yellow film of oil floating on the plate of soup which was proudly placed before her. Next came a dish of brown beans and rice and potatoes cooked in the Portuguese manner, and steak. But the steak was so tough it wore Sarah out trying to chew it, and everything tasted of garlic.

The dessert, however, was better, a sizzling hot platter of banana fritters which Sarah found quite to her liking. She ruined it all by ordering a cup of coffee. This turned out to be the unblended Portuguese type, and was much too strong for her palate.

Considering she might have fared worse, she paid the bill and added a suitable tip, for which the proprietor beamingly dusted off the chairs around her with a tea-stained napkin as she rose to leave. Getting outside wasn't too much of an ordeal, for the café was now half-empty and the men who were left sat dozing over their glasses of wine or mumbling drowsily to their companions.

Once out in the open Sarah staunchly took stock of the situation. She wanted the quickest route back to the hotel. The view of the tiny cobblestoned square with one or two stunted trees and an arched passageway in the corner was not very illuminating. Nevertheless she set forth with her customary fortitude. It was all a question of keeping in the right direction, she told herself, emerging from the passageway and climbing vigorously up yet another alleyway. The fact that she wasn't sure which *was* the right direction could be ignored for the moment.

Occasionally amidst the rooftops of the huddled houses, etched against the deep blue of the afternoon sky, she caught glimpses of the castle on the nearby hill; the same one that she could see from her balcony at the hotel. So things weren't that desperate.

She began to feel a tremor of uncertainty, however, when, several twisting streets and many weary footsteps later, a twilight glow over the rooftops told her that it would soon be dark. Would there ever be any end to the tortuous winding alleys and back-breaking flights of steps?

Still she kept on at a good pace. Nothing would induce her to give up at this stage. Occasionally she would come upon a group of tousled-haired children scuffling outside a doorway, or a plump housewife unpegging the day's washing from a wallside line. It would have been simple enough to ask the way. Even though she spoke no Portuguese she could have mentioned the Avenida da Liberdade. But this would have been admitting that she was in need of help, and Sarah had never been one to do that.

In any case, she reasoned with a clear eye, though her back and legs were aching abominably, these people hadn't spent all their lives living shut away from the rest of the city. They must go out into the sun and the wide streets from time to time, and if they could do it, so could she.

Her tenacity paid off, as she had convinced herself it would, when she rounded a bend which climbed steeply past tall old tile-fronted houses, and there running across the top was a wide boulevard thundering with traffic. It was by now almost dark and everywhere beyond the narrow maze of streets was brilliantly lit. At the top of the hill Sarah stood watching the lights of the cars whizz by, awaiting her chance. And when the green glow of a taxi came into view she waved it to a stop without a qualm. Hang the expense, she told herself, as she tumbled gratefully inside. She could always charge it to the firm, plus her meal if she wanted to; though she wouldn't, of course. It was her own fault she had come so far out of her way, and the oil company paid her far too much anyway.

The mere mention of the Sheraton Hotel brought an energetic show of respect from the taxi-driver, who proceeded to get her there in double-quick time. They whooshed along between the lanes of traffic, attempting some alarming tight squeezes. Not that Sarah was particularly disturbed. She had so many aches and pains she doubted whether she would have noticed if they lost a bumper or two. They were soon back on familiar ground again and it was just as she had suspected, that she had never been far away from the busy thoroughfares throughout her dreary walk.

The tastefully lit entrance of the hotel was a welcome sight. She paid the taxi fare and hobbled across the foyer, past elegantly attired couples, towards the lifts. Upstairs she was sorely tempted to take off her shoes along the carpeted corridor. But that would be undignified. And supposing she met Bryce Taylor?

She wobbled on and coming to her room turned the key in the lock of her door. She noticed with one swift glance that there was no light on in the apartment next door. In the darkness and privacy of her own quarters she kic[illegible] off her shoes and sank wincingly on to the bed. After some considerable time she stirred herself and spent a deliciously long period soaking in a hot bath.

It was getting late when, still stiff, Sarah decided that she had better go and get herself something to eat. She felt a little uncertain about going to the rooftop restaurant on her own, so she went downstairs to the grillroom. It proved to be the worst choice she could have made, being full of hearty, impeccably dressed sporting and tycoon types who gave the room a conservative, hunting lodge atmosphere. She was glad when the ordeal of dining was over so that she could escape back to her room.

She was dragged up from the depths of exhaustion by except to undress and fall into bed. So much for her free day, she smiled grimly to herself as she crawled between the sheets. And as her head touched the pillow she fell instantly asleep.

She was dragged up from the depths of exhaustion by the sound of someone ringing her doorbell. Opening a bleary eye, she saw that it was already daylight. The oil boss's voice came to her through the door. "Time to be on the move, Miss Martindale. We've got quite a bit of business to attend to before we leave for Laso."

Struggling out of the mists of sleep, Sarah called back levelly as though she had been up for hours, "Very well, I'll be there."

She tumbled crossly out of bed and went to take a shower. Couldn't the man have let her sleep in at least until the arrival of the breakfast trolleys? She was dressed ready for the outdoors by the time the waiter rang the bell. But she barely had time to swallow her coffee and rolls before Bryce was ringing again. Confound the man and his impatience! She marched towards the door and flinging it open said crisply, "If you'll just give me time to pack my things."

"Certainly." His mood seemed no better than her own as he stood in the doorway. In his hands he gripped his briefcase and week-end bag. His height and rugged physique came as something of a surprise to Sarah, perhaps because she made it a habit not to notice these things when they were working together.

As she walked about gathering her bits and pieces he

asked with a brusque smile, "Did you have a good day yesterday?"

"Very pleasant, thank you," Sarah said with an offhand air.

Her reply didn't seem to please him all that much. Perhaps he thought she ought to have stayed in her room all day while he was out, *otherwise engaged.* Her feet still throbbed and her legs felt wooden as the result of her disastrous outing, but she took care to show nothing of this as she picked up her bags.

They went out and down in the lift. There was no one to impede their progress across the sumptuous foyer at that time in the morning. Outside, as she stepped into the car, Sarah caught the wisps of perfume lingering over the upholstery, which wasn't her own lavender cologne. She took her seat in frosty silence.

She and Bryce spent an hour calling in at the shops in town and completing small tasks. They had to check that all was in order with the crating and parcelling of their purchases, and arrange for the speediest form of delivery up to the house in Laso. When Sarah closed her notebook at the last shop she thought that was the end of their business in Lisbon. She had forgotten about the staff situation until Bryce brought it to her attention in the car.

"What we need is a couple of first-class chefs to handle the food side, and a good butler," he told her. "The rest of the staff we can engage locally when we need it." They were weaving through the shrieking traffic as he went on, "I'll call in at one or two of the agencies and see what they've got to offer." He surprised Sarah then by adding, "I've made an appointment for you at Casimiros, which I'm told is the best gown shop in town. We're on our way there now. They've got orders to fix you up with a few things."

Sarah fidgeted in her seat and asked icily, "Is that really necessary?"

He replied, swinging into a wide boulevard, "We'll be

entertaining on a lavish scale when we get back. I don't think tweeds are quite the thing to impress the Laso landowners." He pulled up smoothly outside an exclusive fashion house and opening the door for her said energetically, "We want that oil refinery, Miss Martindale."

Sarah got out under sufferance and eyed the opulent frontage. As he cruised away the oil boss told her, "Leave it to them. They know the kind of thing I want. I'll call back and pick you up when I'm through."

Without a backward glance Sarah approached the entrance in haughty manner. If he thought she was going to dress up like his night-club singing lady friend, Miss Maggie la Fay, he was very much mistaken!

She entered the establishment with a sceptical gleam and was immediately seized upon by a dapper little man with a wax-twirled moustache, who seemed to know all about her and why she had called. He led her through the coffee-coloured interior, past white desks and armchairs and cool alabaster columns, clapping his hands with the utmost arrogance. He finally left her with a queenly-looking woman in a black tailored dress, who smilingly took her in hand.

Sarah wasn't remotely interested in fancy clothes and it took her all her time to be civil as she was measured and prepared for the models the vendeuse had lined up for her; garments she was sure were totally unsuitable in every way.

She had to admit to a slight change of heart though when she saw herself later in the mirror. Was that person in the brown silk dress delicately patterned with enormous pink orchids really her? She couldn't believe it; nor that she could feel so at ease in a white flowing dress whose back and front bodice met at the throat in a band of gold and showed an abundance of bare arm.

The vendeuse glided around, obviously pleased with her subject. "So right for Madam's colouring," she would breathe, helping with zips and buckles. Or smoothing out some tailored creation. "This one goes perfectly with Madam's violet eyes."

Sarah was learning a thing or two about herself. Did she really have violet eyes? She had always considered them just a plain and ordinary blue.

She didn't know what orders Bryce Taylor had given, but after the succession of evening wear she found herself trying on elegant summer suits and afternoon dresses. And the vendeuse didn't stop at clothes. Matching shoes were supplied wherever necessary, and Sarah was shown an expensive case of make-up and another one holding jewelled clips and accessories. When she was wearing a white and navy-blue polka-dot two-piece, the woman smiled and complimented her. "The hair style is just right for Madam's face . . . but a little enhancement, perhaps," with which she produced a pair of heavy square-lensed sunglasses. Then draping a vivid pink scarf patterned with white and turquoise stripes over her hair and knotting it loosely under her chin, "For the winds of Portugal, which can be capricious at times."

Sarah gazed at herself under cover of the dark sunglasses. There was no denying the transformation was intriguing. Instead of the overworked secretary she saw a woman, poised and cool, staring back at her from the mirror. A little afraid of this new self she had caught a glimpse of, she wasn't sorry to learn then that the fitting session was over. As quickly as she could, while the garments were being wrapped and boxed ready for delivery along with the other oil company purchases, she departed from the fashion house, secure again in her lavender tweeds.

She had no idea how long Bryce Taylor had been waiting outside in his car, but he looked busy enough with his briefcase open on his knee. When he saw her he gathered his papers together and Sarah took her place beside him with a businesslike air. Her personality might have undergone a subtle change in the luxurious surroundings of

Casimiros, but she had no intention of letting it show.

They set out at once for the outskirts of Lisbon. The day was well on the way to being half over and they still had to get back to Laso. "We'll have to pick up snacks as we go," the oil boss told Sarah when they were speeding along the main highway out of the city. "There's no time for meal breaks."

Sarah was all for keeping moving. She had erected a wall of reserve between herself and Bryce Taylor and this was easier to keep intact while they were racing along. Her books were on the back seat, and she let them stay there. She was still worn out after her marathon walk yesterday and it was a pleasure to just sit and do nothing for once. Later on, towards evening, she had to confess to being guilty of snatching a doze here and there. But she did it so discreetly, sitting perfectly erect in her seat and occasionally letting her eyelids droop, that she was sure Bryce didn't notice. Luckily he showed no desire to switch on the noisy radio.

It was very late when they finally reached Laso. The little harbour town with its flickering lights had a sleepy air after the blaze and clamour of the city. They cruised into the centre. Sarah hardly recognised the embroidery shop in the dim glow of the street lamps, perhaps because she wasn't all that wide awake. She stepped dazedly out of the car.

It was only when she was inside the shop and climbing the stairs to bed that she realised that Bryce had given her a hand with her books and bags and briskly helped her to open the door, before wishing her a brusque goodnight.

CHAPTER SIX

AFTER the Lisbon trip things began to move at a pace. Though the temporary offices down at the wharfside remained in use, the headquarters of the Pyramid Oil Company were transferred to the house on the hill on the outskirts of Laso. The furniture arrived and it was Sarah's job to instruct the army of helpers hired from the town on how to arrange it. She also had to allocate the rooms upstairs according to the staff requirements.

There were offices to be sorted out for herself and the technicians who worked closely with Bryce Taylor. Also the *chef de cuisine*, a Senhor Valadin and his wife, temporarily on loan from the hotel Dom Carlos, and on their way from Lisbon, would require sleeping accommodation on the premises. Eduardo, a tall, thin ascetic-looking individual, who had already arrived to take up butler duties, had arranged his own accommodation in town.

Sarah was kept busy at the house for the best part of each day. Bryce picked her up from the shop in the morning and dropped her off at night. When he wasn't available one of the technicians drove her back. Curiously enough she found she enjoyed being part of a team, and all this bustling activity was, she told herself, just what she needed.

Besides supervising the hanging of pictures or the positioning of antique pieces at the house, there was also her office work. She and Bryce Taylor had the room above the courtyard. It was plastered with maps and project charts and their desks were always littered with papers she hadn't had time to attend to. Whenever she could she stayed on in the evenings to whittle down the piles a little, and as her duties of organising the layout of the house gradually diminished she was able to devote more time to her desk. But, strange as it seemed, it was the mellow interior beyond the office door which occupied most of her thoughts.

It had given her an odd satisfaction to see the rooms of the house taking shape. As often as she could she would stroll with a faint twinge of pride amidst the scenes she had created. Caught up with a constant stream of telex messages from head office, Bryce had been too busy to take much notice of her activities; though she knew that sooner or later he would want to know how the purchases, paid for by the oil company, had been put to use. Still she had an attack of nerves when the inevitable occurred one evening. Supposing he didn't like what she had done?

She was waiting for transport as usual out at the front. The group of technicians, when not exercising their skill with calculating instruments and sea charts, were in the habit of letting off steam in the most noisome manner the moment they hit the outdoors. They were a husky lot and naturally Sarah always kept her distance until she learned which one had been delegated to drive her back to the shop.

Tonight they were indulging in a little friendly horseplay on the drive. The last of the hired hands, engaged for the purposes of tugging with the furniture and arranging the decor around the house, had been paid off in the afternoon and there was a thread of anti-climax in the air at the sense of neatness and order which prevailed. As the oil boss appeared, fastening his suit jacket, a particularly pugnacious member of the group called out, "Hey, boss! When are you going to invite us to dinner? The new pad looks great."

"The idea is to promote good relations in the town, not scare the local population out of its wits," Bryce replied drily.

Sarah noticed he could joke and smile with his men in an easy way. With her he had taken to wearing an air of brusque formality which matched entirely her own austere businesslike approach.

"I haven't had time to see how the place looks." He turned to gaze about him, and a crack showed in his urbanity as he suggested, "Perhaps Miss Martindale would do the honours?"

The men, enjoying his dry mood, took themselves off, whooping and laughing, to their cars. They drove off noisily and Sarah was left with the unenviable task of showing Bryce around.

They walked inside and feeling ridiculously knotted up Sarah said in high-pitched tones, "Shall we start with the main lounge?"

She led the way across the red-tiled hall where the leaves of an exotic plant, gleaming in its copper container, warmed a bare corner, and into the room opposite. The walk-in fireplace was furnished with chintz-padded seats and coffee tables and a huge white skin rug fronted the log fire centrepiece. Around the room polished tables and sideboards reflected the blue of the sky and the greenery of the garden through the windows. As the day was coming to a close the reflections were tinged with a glow of amber. There was an abundance of armchairs arranged beside lamps and antique pieces, and huge velvet sofas, themselves a warm amber, played a dominant part in the centre of the room.

Though Sarah was all too conscious of Bryce viewing everything with his keen eye beside her, she, oddly enough, felt considerably less tense in the peaceful glow. After a few moments she moved on towards the rest of the ground-floor rooms, past a waist-high sculpture of a man on horseback in the hall which they had picked up in Lisbon, and on to gather glimpses of lilac walls and lime green interiors and window recesses curtained in tasteful designs.

The smaller rooms were more intimate, the large room designed expressly for entertaining was more animated with its tapestry wall hangings and old-world flavour. As the house had been bought strictly for business purposes, only two or three of the rooms upstairs had been furnished as bedrooms. The rest were offices cluttered with measuring machinery and drawing paraphernalia which didn't need to be touched on.

Bryce had said nothing during their tour and coming back down to the hall again Sarah felt her heart banging rather painfully. What did he think? She was terribly aware of the sound of his shoes clicking over the polished red tiles of the hall as he strolled. And then he said as he walked about, "Supposing we put the horseman over there ... and push the refectory table a little closer to the wall, about here ... to create more space, don't you think?"

Sarah inclined her head. "It does look better." She felt the tension leave her and a peculiar golden light flood into her heart. Bryce Taylor wasn't a man to demonstrate his feelings, but she knew by his actions and the dark flush of pleasure on his face that he approved of her ideas.

Dusk was shrouding the grounds when they went outside. The warmth of summer was in the air and on the stillness one could hear the roll of the sea down below the belt of eucalyptus trees. Sarah locked the door of the house. When she turned Bryce was strolling beside the patio garden with its climbing roses. He breathed in the fragrance from the flower-beds and tree plots, newly dug over by the army of gardeners, and with an unusual show of expansiveness he stated, "Well, Miss Martindale, I think O Saudade is ready to be opened to the public."

"I beg your pardon . . . O? . . ." Sarah looked blank.

"O Saudade," he repeated with the suggestion of a lazy gleam in his green eyes. "It's the name of the house. I found out yesterday."

It was growing dark, so Sarah couldn't be sure, but she thought the oil man gave her a searching look as he asked casually, "How does it strike you?"

"It's . . . beautiful . . ." Sarah couldn't hold back the

word. Then to cover up this unusual lapse of emotion in her, she added crisply, "But I don't care for the expression 'open to the public'. It sounds like a stately home on its last legs."

"On a minor scale, that's what it was, I believe, until a French count had it restored." Bryce led the way out to the car beyond the green gates.

But Sarah couldn't resist a look back. "O Saudade." She said the name as the oil boss had pronounced it, Sah-oo-dard, and asked, "What does it mean?"

"It's a favourite word of the Portuguese, literally meaning *yearning*."

Yearning. A strange thrill rippled through Sarah as she stared at the jutting gables and sloping rooftops of the house, silhouetted against the fire of the dying day. She kept her gaze riveted there because for some ridiculous reason after the oil boss's reply she didn't know where else to put it.

As though he too felt a peculiar awkwardness in the moment he hurried on, with a great show of ease, "As a nation with a dwindling empire they nurse a nostalgia for something lost that perhaps was never really there."

Like him Sarah made an effort to appear relaxed; though it was difficult. This was the most they had said to one another, apart from the usual business talk, since their dinner together at the rooftop restaurant in Lisbon.

To regain firm ground she turned and said with a matter-of-fact air, "And now the house is to be opened to visitors."

"That's what we bought it for," the oil man smiled a little cynically as he glanced over it. "A sprat to catch a mackerel. A fish in the form of some of the shrewdest businessmen in town, and worth its weight in diamonds if we can hook it." He opened the car door for Sarah and climbing in beside her he added, "Tomorrow we'll send out the invitation cards and start the ball rolling with a few top names. Wednesday of next week, I think, would be a good night for the first oil company reception."

Sarah made a note of the date and the car started away. They were back to business again.

She spent the next few days in a state of trepidation. Her hostessing role was drawing near and she hadn't the faintest idea how she was going to cope in the staged and moneyed atmosphere of the oil world. Thank goodness there was plenty to do to take her mind off her worries.

With Bryce Taylor she made out a list of the most influential people and typed out the invitations as he strode around wording the cards in his own way. She noticed that each message had a personal friendly touch as though he was already well acquainted with the people who mattered in the town.

Afterwards she toured the house with him making notes as efficiently as she could of his other requests. There were flowers for all the rooms to be ordered for delivery on the day in question, and taped music to be played wherever possible. The chef and his wife arrived from the hotel in town and Sarah had to smooth them down because the kitchen wasn't as big as the ones they had been used to working in. Eduardo, already a fixture on the premises during the day, strolled around looking suitably noncommittal and elegant. It was left to him to engage the various house staff required for the evening.

The larders had to be stocked and it was Sarah's job to check the contents of the delivery vans against the chef's lists. As she was often still busy at the end of the day she found it more convenient to use a bedroom on the premises than keep going backwards and forwards to the shop. Also the arrangement suited her in other ways. She had never cared for the coarse humour and somewhat reckless driving of the technicians, yet lately she found herself equally ill at ease when being driven home by Bryce.

The gowns and other apparel ordered for her from Casimiros had arrived and in the spare moments in her room she would finger through them nervously. She clung tenaciously to her tweed suits, though after weeks of constant use it was obvious that they would soon have to be replaced by other garments.

The offices were closed on the day of the oil company reception. The technicians were working down at the harbour and Sarah had nothing to do until the evening when the guests would arrive. The chef was now providing the meals. She found it rather strange lunching in the sunny dining room with Bryce and being waited upon by the smooth and polished Eduardo. To maintain a sense of balance she kept her pad and pencil at the side of her plate so that she could refer to her notes whenever the oil boss mentioned a point.

Upstairs in her room after the meal the afternoon yawned before her. She was not used to having so much time on her hands. Also she felt edgy when she thought of the evening to come. It only made matters worse when some time later she went downstairs and round to the loggia with a book to find Bryce sitting there deep in a newspaper. A little startled himself, he rose to his feet at once when he saw her.

If Sarah had been the type of person who could pass off a difficult moment she would have sat down and calmly opened her book. But she wasn't. She felt the suffocating colour of shyness envelope her at her blunder. This made her voice sound cold as she said with a flustered air, "I'm sorry, I didn't know you were here."

"Don't apologise." The oil man, looking unusually relaxed in pale slacks and woollen sweater, cast a dry gleam around the leafy area with its comfortable cane-work chairs and added, "I think there's room enough for two."

Room there might have been, but the air had become, nonetheless, somewhat stifling. Sarah clutched her book to her and edged away. "Please don't disturb yourself," she said hurriedly, trying to sound politely apologetic, "I'll . . . er . . . I'll go for a walk . . ." Quickly she disappeared round the side of the house.

She had no idea where she was going to walk, but was too afraid to stop now, so she kept going along the paths until she came to the gates on the edge of the grounds. Outside, the road curved away round the shoulder of the hill towards town. At the side of the road the eucalyptus forests sloped down towards the sea. Feeling a sudden desire to know the freedom of the beach, Sarah set off a little recklessly through the trees and down the steep incline. She always wore stout shoes, and though there were no paths and the soil was dry and crumbly so that from time to time she had to clutch at a sapling to keep her balance, she made excellent progress.

She was perhaps spurred on by a curious lighthearted feeling. Still lingering in her mind was the picture of Bryce's green eyes gleaming at her in an almost humorous fashion. The memory had a stimulating effect on her so that she arrived at the bottom of the incline without having noticed much of the hazards of the trip.

The beach was a golden yellow, the sand smooth and unmarred by footprints. The salt spray from the gentle Atlantic breakers down on this lonely stretch, mingled with the sharp warm tang of eucalyptus and pine trees. Sarah had never been one to pay much attention to her surroundings, but just lately she had been discovering worlds other than her desk.

This afternoon she wanted to go on looking at the view; at the sea, the foaming waves and the glistening blue-green swell stretching into the far distance, and at the hillside, the houses simple in line and colour-washed, on the way to town, the white villas amidst their smother of blossom looking south.

Immediately above she could see the rooftops of O Saudade. The once red tiles were bleached into a pale russet by the long summers of fierce sun. How strange to think that such a beautiful old house was now being used for business purposes; that half its rooms had been turned into offices, and the people working in it were part of a huge impersonal combine.

If Bryce Taylor had been a married man, of course, things would have been different. There would have been no offices at O Saudade and with a wife beside him he would have entertained in their home, combining business with pleasure, like so many couples the world over. Sarah knew that several of the technicians were renting houses along the coast with their wives. But the oil boss belonged to the bachelor world of shrewd business dealings and oil company assignments, Sarah mused towards the white-capped ocean. His job in Laso was to win the hearts of the local people and he was depending solely on her, his personal assistant, to help him do it.

She watched the incoming swell shot with the rainbow rays of the sun, and the twinkling wavelets spend themselves as dark stains upon the sand. She felt the sea-wind plucking at wisps of hair around her face disturbing her usual orderly appearance. Its keeness brought a brilliance to her eyes. She was lost in the gentle roar, carried away on the rushing surf which tugged and heaved before her, when a sudden crashing sound from behind made her turn quickly.

As the figure of the oil boss appeared it was Sarah's turn to look startled. A lock of dark hair had fallen over his brow with the effort of steering his big frame down the steep incline. He said somewhat churlishly, in those tones he used when he was slightly put out, "When you said you were going for a walk, I thought you meant for ten minutes in the grounds. I've been looking for you, to gen me up on the anti-pollution laws."

Sarah was a little surprised at his words. As far as she knew she was free from her duties until this evening. And he had certainly given her no indication earlier that he would need her for anything. Also he must have watched her from the house at the start of her descent to know which way she had come. But she replied levelly enough,

"I'll search out the information in the files for you, when I get back."

The oil boss steadied himself and shot a glance up through the trees. "This is a dangerous route to take down here," he said, brushing himself off. "If you'd asked me I could have told you, there's a private way down to the beach from the house." He stretched up to his full height and ran a hand through his hair, and pointing up the curve of the beach towards the far side of the forest slope he added casually, "Now that I'm here I might as well show you the way."

The walk took about twenty minutes. For once Sarah felt no inhibitions at the close proximity of the oil boss. With the blue sparkle of the sky and the excitement of the tumbling waves, she was filled with a strange new sense of freedom. As the two of them swung along over the firm sand at the water's edge there suddenly seemed no need for business chat or the wielding of pad and pencil. It was enough to hear the crisp crunching of their footsteps mingling with the rustle of the wind. She arrived a little breathless at the end of their walk, though she tried not to show it by gazing back at their two sets of tracks along the virgin stretch of sand.

The private walk up the craggy slope to the house consisted of little flights of steps and clusters of flower-sprinkled rockeries. In leafy arbours looking out to sea there were stone seats tiled in the Portuguese *azulejos*, and spiky green palms clung to the soil.

Sarah had to keep making the excuse of stopping to look at the view, for the way was steep and she couldn't disguise her breathlessness. Bryce, obviously finding it little effort, waited with her and looked at the view too. When they were almost at the top he pointed over her shoulder. "There's Laso, round the headland. And you can just see the oil refinery site beyond the harbour."

Sarah gazed at the distant rolling stretches of scrubland. "And someone owns all that?" she asked, trying not to notice the sweater-clad arm alongside her cheek.

"A handful of wealthy families," he replied. And with the old dryness in his voice, "But we're hoping to change all that. It's my job to convince them that an extremely healthy bank account can be a lot more useful than a few acres of infertile land." He looked at his watch and as though thinking of the evening to come, said, "We'd better get on. It will be dark in an hour."

The steps led them into an orchard in a sheltered hollow of the grounds. From here they followed the path which brought them out to the ornamental fruit trees bordering the lawn. Across in the loggia Sarah could see the oil boss's newspaper still open where he had left it on a chair. As they went indoors he made no mention of the anti-pollution information he had asked her for earlier.

At nine o'clock the cars started to thunder up. They parked in the grounds and on the roadside, outside the gates. The house was ablaze with lights which spilled out over the gardens and tree-clad slopes. Sarah was up in her room trembling slightly as she applied a brush of powder to her cheeks, a touch of pale colour to her lips. She had searched out the most unobtrusive of the Casimiro creations, a coffee-coloured gown with a matching rose at the waist. Her hair, smooth and pale over her brow, was caught into a golden knob at the back and held by a jewelled clasp.

She fretted over her appearance and walked before the mirror a dozen times. Then realising she could no longer put off the fateful moment she went downstairs. If only she had known how easy it was all going to be she could have saved herself endless moments of anxiety. No one thought there was anything the least odd in her apparel. As she swept through the brilliantly-lit rooms attending to last-minute details the hired staff eyed her respectfully. And when she went to see that all was well in the serving pantry and kitchens she won a look of approval from the stately Eduardo, himself immaculate in dark tails.

The guests started to percolate into the rooms and knowing that her place was with Bryce Taylor Sarah hurried to assist him, at the front door. There was no awkwardness in her arrival, for the agony of looking different had quickly flown in the normality of her surroundings. Her equilibrium was upset only slightly when she glimpsed Bryce's big frame in a strikingly well-cut suit with a dark blue sheen on it, and in turn felt his green gaze swing round momentarily and fasten on her approach. But smiling couples were coming in from the night and Sarah found herself smiling too in reply, and Bryce was shaking hands and welcoming the flow of people and saying in an incredibly relaxed way amidst all the happy chatter and introductions ". . . and this is my personal assistant, Miss Martindale."

Nothing seemed more natural to Sarah after that than to go attending to the guests' needs, helping out where she could at the buffet tables which were filled with delicacies of every kind, seeing that the wine glasses were kept topped up on the waiters' trays, and that no one was left alone in a corner without a partner to talk to. She knew that the guest lists had been arranged to include only a handful of the people important to Pyramid Oil, and there was certainly nothing to suggest business in the gay party atmosphere, though she thought she detected the oil boss's subtle approach at times as he stood chatting with couples here and there around the room. His was strictly a man's world, but Sarah noticed he could make himself pleasant with women when he wanted to, as he had done with Maggie la Fay in Lisbon, she thought with a queer stab inside.

Working so close to Bryce all these weeks Sarah had deliberately kept him as a shadowy figure in her mind. But tonight she felt disinclined to enforce this rigid rule. Instead, when she could, she let her gaze linger on the width of his shoulders, the way his eyebrows sloped down at the sides when he smiled.

On one of these occasions when she had been thus engrossed she was aware vaguely of undergoing the same treatment herself. Mingling with the guests, exchanging a smiling word here and there, she had not been entirely blind to the appraising glances that had followed her from time to time. But the man whose eyes met hers across the room when she turned on this occasion struck her as being the type she wouldn't want to regard as a friend.

He was probably about thirty and had the kind of bearing which suggested arrogance. His aquiline features might have been described as handsome but for a swarthiness in his complexion. He wore his black hair untidily long. Sarah noticed that he watched her every move as she strolled around, with eyes lustrously dark and broodingly speculative.

She had never been looked at in quite that way by a man before, and she wasn't sure that she cared for it. Though he was probably an important member of the Laso community and as such was entitled to her attention, she went out of her way to avoid him.

Around twelve the gathering started to break up. Cigars were left smoking to themselves in the ashtrays and wraps were collected from the adjoining rooms. Car headlights beamed over the house as one by one they swung away down the hillside and back to town. Indoors the hired staff were left with the job of clearing away the punch bowls and trays scattered over the tables, the empty wine glasses and food plates littering the rooms.

The chef, Senhor Valadin, and his wife, a couple with the kind of glowing pink faces that have spent much time over bubbling saucepans and sizzling hot grills, came out to bask in the faded glory of their labours. Proudly they supervised the scant left-overs back to the kitchen. They were standing in the hall with Sarah, chattering excitedly about the popularity of their royal Romanoff cake which they had been unable to supply fast enough, when Bryce Taylor came through ready to leave. He looked pleased with the evening and standing for a moment to button his jacket against the night air, he said with his old buoyancy, "Well, I think we've shown the Laso people we're ready to meet them on any level. Let's hope it won't be long before we have them eating out of our hands." He smiled around briefly and with a nod Sarah's way, "Good-night, Miss Martindale," he strode away to his car. Sarah went up to her room feeling drowsily content.

She had no qualms about entertaining after that. In fact she came to look forward to the frequent gatherings at O Saudade, subtly arranged of course to coincide with some public holiday or local event in Laso. Sometimes there was a fair-sized crowd made up of the local dignitaries and influential people in the district, as on that first night. At others, there was just a handful of people, wharf-owners and property men, vital to Pyramid Oil.

But Sarah knew nothing about that. Her job was simply to make the guests feel at home, and this she did as second nature. She was learning a lot about herself since joining Pyramid Oil. She had never thought herself capable of acting the role of hostess, yet here she was combining her office duties through the week with those of organising the hospitality at O Saudade when the occasion arose.

As the weather grew warmer, small cocktail parties became a feature of the outdoors. On a week-end afternoon the buffet tables could be seen under gay awnings in the garden and the guests wandered over the lawns clad in summer apparel. Sometimes one or two of the technicians and their wives came to mingle with the invited assembly to add normality to the scene.

For the sun Sarah would put on an elegant linen suit, or a tailored summer dress, without thinking twice about the poised picture she presented. She learned to drape a colourful string of beads with a plain open-necked blouse, and to tie an expensive scarf at her throat to combat the whisper of a cool breeze. She would stand talking alongside the oil boss, unaware of the smooth outline of her brow, and profile against the sunlight, the graceful curve of her throat.

She loved to hear the Portuguese talk. They had imported the quaint old-world English used for centuries amongst the wine shippers in the district, and it was a delight to hear the language spoken as it should be. The businessmen chatted away and joked quite fluently; their wives, a little more conscious of their accents, were a little shyer of joining in the conversation. It was up to Sarah to draw them out where she could.

Sometimes Bryce Taylor was missing from the group and Sarah would spot him across the garden engaged in an earnest discussion with a member of the gathering, no doubt someone useful to Pyramid Oil. Wherever he was her eyes would always find him, and not infrequently he would raise his for a moment and follow her in passing. Whenever she could she would let her gaze linger on his tall lightly-clad frame, and her heart would sing a little song.

CHAPTER SEVEN

DURING the week, except on public holidays, the oil company offices on the upper floor of O Saudade continued to function normally. All the staff were officially compelled to take one day off in five, and this included Sarah, who invariably had her free day mid-week. She was quite content to spend it tidying her room, or strolling in the grounds now drenched with colour and perfumed with the fragrance of blossoming shrubs, or down at the beach. But occasionally, if the chef and his wife were having an afternoon in town, she would beg a lift in order to do a little personal shopping.

One June afternoon, leaving the busy sound of the clicking telex, men's voices and buzzing telephones drifting from the upstairs windows, she climbed into the couple's rather dated Citroen bound for Laso. Senhor Valadin and his wife were a comfortable pair. Their work was considered of international standard and they had seen service in some of the most exclusive hotels in Europe. Lucia Valadin loved to tell the story of the feud in the Paris kitchens when she had refused to work with the chef put in charge, and had once chased him with a meat chopper before they finally settled their differences over a wedding breakfast of *bacalhou a Bras*.

Now they were a successful partnership working mainly in Portugal. They didn't think there was anything the least odd in loaning their services out to Pyramid Oil, and preparing succulent displays to further the oil company's image in town. Every new engagement was an adventure to them, and though they were as temperamental as two prima donnas when viewing their place of employment for the first time, it was clear that they rather enjoyed the feeling of not knowing what was going to happen next. It was Lucia who did most of the talking on the car trips into town. The couple spent their free time gossiping with the friends they had made at the pavement café tables.

They dropped Sarah off in the usual place, in the little square where the bus parked, and arranged to pick her up there at seven for the return trip. She looked at her watch as they drove away. It was only a little bit after three, so she had ample time to pick up her bits and pieces of shopping. She was in no hurry this afternoon. The sun was shining and the little harbour town was alive with that kind of activity which comes from being situated near the sea. There was the scent of sawn wood in the air and fishwomen carrying their baskets of glistening sardines and plaice uttered the strangest cries; harsh almost wooden chants which changed suddenly into the most melodious of notes. There were knife-grinders too, whistling tunes almost oriental in their approach, and from the stalls lining the side streets, the cries of vendors of all manner of eatables could be heard.

Sarah was wearing a salmon-coloured suit with a striped scarf at her throat. Her heart was light and it felt good just walking and soaking up the sights and sounds. They were scenes that at one time would have passed her eye unnoticed, but which today seemed somehow edged with gold.

She wandered past the cool and cleanly-coloured houses into the busy shopping section. Here the animation was of a different kind; of striding Portuguese businessmen, black-shawled women and plump housewives with heavy gold medallions on their chests, pushing into the stores and jostling one another on the pavement. Sarah mingled with the crush.

She had bought herself some new cologne, and was gazing at a display of local pottery in a shop window when she felt a hand grip her lightly on the arm and a voice said in low tones in her ear, "*Boa tarde*, Senhorita Martindale. Your presence is requested at the Quinta."

Sarah felt the strength drain away from her. She turned quickly to stare in shocked surprise at the thick-set man in neat blue suit standing close to her. She barely recognised him out of uniform. It was the Carvalhos' chauffeur.

She couldn't think clearly. Playing for time, she said, trying to sound pleasant, "Of course! I'll make a trip out there some time."

But as she turned away the grip on her arm tightened. "I think Senhor Carvalho would prefer you to come now." The voice was firm and Sarah had no choice but to let herself be led away. She was guided discreetly through the mêlée of shoppers and away into a side street where she was helped into a waiting car and transported silently away. It all happened so quickly, her abduction in the crowded centre went by unnoticed.

As the car headed for the outskirts of town Sarah sat on the back seat, her heart thudding rapidly. It was two months since she had left the Carvalhos' estate that night to take up residence at the embroidery shop, and a lot had happened since then. Working for the oil company, she had gradually found herself hoping that nothing would come of the Carvalhos' plan to contact her. Her decision to lock up the shop and transfer her personal possessions to O Saudade had been made partly out of a desire to escape. As the weeks had gone by without a word or a sign from the Quinta she had begun to feel optimistic. She had even fooled herself into believing that the wine family must have dropped their idea of trying to compete with the oil company.

What a mistake that had been! They had obviously been keeping tabs on her all the time and knew her every move, judging by the way their chauffeur had known exactly where to find her in Laso. She took a quivering breath and sat back glumly. Well, she was on the way to the Quinta now, so there was nothing to be done but to get the visit over with as quickly as possible.

She turned her eye to the view, wondering why she had

never noticed the colossal beauty of the drive on that first run. The road curved and clung to the shoulders of towering hillsides thick with forests of cork trees and pines. It would plunge into ravines starred with wild flowers and rise to a sky of scudding white clouds near enough to touch. There was the scent of lavender and sage in the air and the ever-present salt tang of the sea.

Coming into the Amorida valley the road snaked through the terraced vineyards. The vines were in full leaf, rich and green and glossy with promise. In the distance the amber walls of the Quinta were etched against the hillside. Sarah felt her nerves tighten up as the car purred in through the gates. She experienced that feeling once again of being a prisoner, once they were inside the battlement-type walls surrounding the property. The car skirted the ornamental gardens and slid up alongside the steps fronting the house.

Sarah was helped out of her seat with all the pomp befitting a celebrity. Exuding that polished air, in a fawn-coloured suit and white shirt, Senhor Carvalho was waiting on the steps to greet her, as she knew he would be. "Good afternoon, Miss Martindale." His welcome was warm and friendly. He wasn't in the least put out by Sarah's frigid reception. Indicating the door, he said with his usual sweeping air, "Shall we go inside?" And as they passed through and into the hall he commented gallantly, leading the way to his office, "May I say you're looking very well?"

Sarah made no reply. She was thinking of the last time she had wandered through this gracious old house, with its ornate rooms and ancestral heritage. What a different person she had been then! Gone now were her dowdy tweed suits and cloche hats. And she hadn't thought of Mr. Grapplewick in weeks.

There was no sign of the other members of the family. The sons were probably out working in the fields, and the daughters looking after their small children somewhere.

From the businesslike gleam in Senhor Carvalho's dark eyes as he closed the office door behind them, Sarah had the feeling they had been told to make themselves scarce.

She perched on the edge of the same chair as she had done last time. The wine-grower took his place behind the desk and clasping his hands on the blotter he said with an anticipatory air, "Now! You have much to report, have you not?"

Sarah tried to look vague and hedged coldly, "Very little, I'm afraid."

"Oh, come now!" Senhor Carvalho leaned back good-naturedly. "We know there has been much activity at the refinery site, and at the company headquarters out of town." He reached into a drawer at the side of his desk and startled Sarah by producing a property map almost identical to the one on the wall in the oil office.

It brought her to her feet and as she stared at the familiar numbered sections Senhor Carvalho smiled and tapped a finger in the harbour area. "Rumour has it that the shipwright brothers, the Oliveitas, have capitulated to the oil company. Is this true?"

Though the wine-grower had lost none of his charm Sarah felt impaled by the ruthlessness in his gaze. "I . . . think they've settled on a price," she admitted reluctantly.

"And the municipal authorities. Have they agreed on compensation for the old civic site on the south bank?"

"It's still under consideration. There's to be a meeting on the first of the month."

Skilfully Senhor Carvalho wrung out of Sarah what he wanted to know. It was information that only she and Bryce Taylor had access to. Rapidly he worked with a pencil, criss-crossing sections and scribbling comments in the margins. After half an hour the aspect of the map had changed considerably. Senhor Carvalho, however, was unperturbed.

"Mr. Taylor still has a long way to go." He studied the map carefully, then rolled it up with an air of satisfaction.

"From what I hear there is still a lot of opposition in the town concerning the oil refinery. At the moment it appears we have little to worry about." He put the map away and locking the drawer dropped the key into his pocket. "Now! would you like to take tea?"

He was back to his usual expansive manner and one would have thought they had merely been discussing a change in the weather.

"If you don't mind I'd rather get straight back to town," Sarah said in a drained voice. How distasteful she had found the last half hour. Though, in coming here, she had only done what she had agreed to do at the start, she felt unclean in some way. She was filled with an urge to get quickly away from the Quinta.

"Very well," Senhor Carvalho agreed in affable tones. "I'll ring for Januario at once." Having done so he walked with her across the room. Then he took her limp hand in a suave farewell. "Goodbye, Miss Martindale. I trust you'll make yourself available to us, should the necessity arise."

As they waited for the chauffeur to appear Sarah found her gaze wandering along with his to a crest above the doorway. Inscribed on it in gilt letters were the words *Sempre leal*.

"It's the family motto," Senhor Carvalho explained. "Always loyal." He turned to give her a shrewd twinkle.

Sarah went out with a painful flush on her cheeks.

She remembered little of the ride back to town. Her mind was in a torment after the events of the afternoon. Vaguely she was aware of the winding road beneath the wheels of the car and the steady hum of the engine. But their arrival in Laso was lost on her, and it came as a mild shock to find the chauffeur holding the door for her in a deserted alley on the fringe of the town centre.

She still had half an hour or so before meeting the Valadins. Nervously she picked up one or two items of shopping mainly to avoid arousing suspicion, and pleading a headache she sat in silence on the drive back to O Saudade.

The next day was a bad one for Sarah. She couldn't work for the feeling of guilt which dogged her. Everything she touched in the oil offices seemed to be a reminder of the conversation she had had with Senhor Carvalho at the Quinta; the property map on the wall which she was constantly having to re-locate with coloured flags, the letters from the local governing authorities which she had to file or type out replies to. Stiff with tension she went about these tasks awkwardly, making blunders at every turn. As she picked her pencil up for the third time during the course of dictating a letter, Bryce Taylor joked, "You're as nervous as a new office girl this morning, Miss Martindale. Is anything the matter?"

"No.... Oh no! Nothing at all." Sarah tried to smile brightly over the suffocating thudding of her heart.

Towards the week-end her shredded nerves had healed over enough to cope with the latest informal gathering spilling over the lawns of O Saudade. Outwardly serene, she might have found the afternoon blissfully uneventful but for the unsettling presence of the saturnine figure with the black smouldering eyes who was always turning up at these functions. There was something about his latin looks and manner that repulsed Sarah and ever since that first night she had given him a wide berth, though she was not unaware that he spent his time angling for a conversation with her.

She was still shaky inside, and his insolent brooding gaze trailing her everywhere, put her on edge this afternoon. She chose a moment when he was engaged in conversation to find out more about him.

"Eduardo," she touched the sleeve of the butler as he was passing by with his tray. "Who is that man over there? The slim one talking to the civic engineer"

The Portuguese manservant followed her gaze and informed her discreetly, "That is Senhor Jacinto Douro, madam."

"Does he live in Laso?" Sarah asked.

"No, the family wine business is in Vila Nova da Gaia across the river, but I believe he has important connections in the town."

"Thank you, Eduardo." Sarah nodded the butler on his way. Knowing the man's name and occupation wasn't much help and she wondered if, after all, he had not been entirely unaware of her whispered enquiry, for later, when she was standing beside Bryce, he contrived to make himself a member of the group they were chatting to and despite Sarah's coolness she found him kissing her hand with a sly gleam in his eyes.

His English was faultless, though he spoke it with the condescension befitting his arrogant stance; which was odd, for though his bearing suggested breeding there was nothing polished about his appearance. Sarah had plenty of opportunity to study him while he discussed the aspects of the refinery with the oil boss.

His hair was untidily long in the modern cult. He was unconventionally dressed in a white sweater with a huge polo neck which showed slackly beneath a dark jacket and a cape. The cape gave him a slight flair which he used to advantage in gaining the attention of the rest of the group. He didn't possess the maturity of having made his way on his own and Sarah suspected it was family connections in Laso which gave him his status.

It was obvious from his conversation that he supported the idea of the oil refinery, almost enthusiastically so. This made him invaluable to Pyramid Oil. Yet Sarah had the feeling that Bryce shared her dislike of the man. Even so, when, after speaking at length with a fierce pride of the family business, Senhor Douro said to him with a hooded look at Sarah, "You and your charming assistant must come and visit our wine cellars some time," the oil boss accepted the invitation readily.

"Miss Martindale and I will be only too glad to come and sample the contents of the barrels," he joked with that lopsided smile of his. "How about tomorrow? We've got a free day."

Had they? Sarah wasn't aware of it.

"Excellent," the young Portuguese bowed over her hand. As the party broke up Sarah left the two men discussing the arrangements for the visit. She wasn't at all happy about the trip. There was a fire behind Jacinto Douro's gaze when he looked at her which bothered her.

Bryce called for Sarah about mid-morning the next day. She quite forgot her misgivings of the day before when she saw him, big in a light grey summer suit, though she was careful not to let her happiness show. She was wearing an oatmeal-coloured dress with large patch pockets and a wide belt hugging her slim waist. For a touch of colour she had experimented and settled for a pair of amber ear-rings and a matching lipstick.

Bryce held the car door for her, knocking his pipe on the side in that way of his when he was not completely at ease. Inside the car an air of reserve settled between them, as it always did when they were away from the work scene. Driving out of the gates of O Saudade and down the steep road, he said, seemingly at pains to sound offhand, "I thought we'd make a day of it and see something of Porto while we're down that way."

Sarah resisted the urge to reply in her office tones, "Very well," and managed instead an unemotional, "That sounds like a good idea."

That was the extent of their conversation, but with the sun shining like spun gold through the ragged eucalyptus trees and the sea beckoning in the distance, Sarah preferred the peace anyway, and somehow she felt that Bryce did too.

In such a mood they drove down to Porto and wandered around its colourful riverside quarters. They visited its monuments and strolled along the banks of the Douro river to watch the curious barges or *rabelos* that carried the port wine down from the vineyards. They drove out to Foy do Douro where the river so picturesquely joined hands with the ocean, and later sampled the city's gastronomical specialities in an open loggia restaurant with a view of the port.

It was after three when Bryce said with a glance at his watch, as they returned to the car, "The port lodges should have resumed business again by now after the midday break."

Sarah had quite forgotten their appointment at Vila Nova da Gaia. She was in no way looking forward to the trip and would have been content to drive slowly back through the cool green woods, skirting the tiny fishing villages and golden stretches of beach, to O Saudade.

They drove to the south bank across the river Douro, crossing the Dom Luis bridge, a network of steel which cast its giant shadow upon the yellow water below. Vila Nova da Gaia was a cluster of sleepy white houses and tree-shaded walks. The ancient port lodges of the wine merchants hugged the riverside amidst a scattering of barrels, barges and loading jetties. The older houses close to the river were mellowed stone affairs with lopsided shutters at the windows and flowerpots around the doorways. Here and there a wooden handcart rested on its shafts beneath a slender leafy tree.

The lodge of Manoel da Douro and Burminster had its entrance off one of these streets. As Bryce parked the car in the shady cul-de-sac Jacinto Douro came out from the lodge to meet them. Sarah was no nearer to liking the egotistical Portuguese on this second meeting. He was wearing a dark suit, a little too tight for his slim frame, and an open-necked pink shirt, the collar of which flapped untidily around his dark locks. Sarah could imagine that his conquests with the opposite sex were numerous, for he had the strut of a man who knows his value with women.

Though he kept his eyes on the oil boss while he greeted them profusely she had the feeling that he was watching her from the tail end of his gaze.

They went inside and down wooden steps below the offices. Later the steps were of stone and went round in a horseshoe as they descended into a cavern-like interior. Sarah shivered slightly, though her reaction was not entirely due to the curtain of cold air which met them. The gloom oppressed her and she saw nothing attractive in racks of barrels stretching as far as the eye could see beneath old stone archways and a fluted roof. However, she had to remember that they were being favoured with a conducted tour and she pretended to listen attentively as the son of the firm gave a history of the business as he led them around.

There were men in white coats moving along the aisles with ladles and trays of glasses, professional tasters, Sarah learned, as their host told them in his autocratic tones. "Tasters," he said, "seldom really taste. We first check the colour by holding a glass of wine against the light." He whipped a glass from a taster's hand without so much as a "do you mind" to demonstrate. "Then we swirl it to observe the qualities of the froth and finally inhale the bouquet. Only if some doubt remains," he thrust the glass back into the man's hand and walked on, "do we actually sample a wine. And a taster merely uses his tongue and the roof of his mouth. He never swallows."

He passed a couple of men in overalls rolling barrels up a ramp as though they weren't there and went on, "Our farms are known as *quintas*. Many farmers sell their grapes direct to the shippers. The old custom of trampling the wine-press," he waved an arm airily to an antique press in the shadows, "belongs to the past. When our grapes are brought to the *quinta* they are poured into a *lagar* in which they are crushed by machinery. Later brandy is added to stop the process of fermentation."

As he talked and walked Bryce Taylor took a lazy

interest in his surroundings and occasionally stopped to examine a metal tag on a barrel or to run a hand over the ancient timber racks.

"We started mixing brandy with our wine in the seventeenth century," they were told by their host. "We were joined about that time by our British partners, Burminsters of London. Since then the port wine of the house of Manoel Douro has reigned supreme."

Sarah thought of the Carvalhos and the special privileges they enjoyed in the Amorida valley. Judging from the activity she had seen down at the Laso harbour where their wine was shipped abroad, there was no doubt they were high on the list of world exporters. She said smoothly with a desire to prick Jacinto Douro's puffed-up pride, "Surely there are others who also claim that distinction?"

As though he too was thinking of the Carvalhos their host's nostrils flared and he said in tones laced with scorn, "There are those who grow their grapes in inferior regions and fool themselves into thinking that their wine is superior to all others." He snorted proudly. "But it is the port wine of the Douro's from the Douro slopes—we even took our name from the river—which gains favour at home and abroad."

Sarah made no further comment and pretended to be greatly interested in the leather-bound visitors' book on top of an ancient bureau. But the younger Douro's arrogant retort had given her something to think about. Though no names had been mentioned, there was no doubt in her mind that his scorn had been directed at the Amorida valley concern. It was obvious that there was fierce competition between the two firms. It struck Sarah that the Douro family could be the rivals the Carvalhos had spoken of.

As Jacinto Douro continued with his tour Sarah watched him speculatively. It was an interesting theory. It would explain why he was so enthusiastic about having the oil refinery at Laso. If Pyramid Oil took over the harbour the Carvalhos would be squeezed out of the port wine trade. That would leave the way clear for the Douros to take over the lead.

She lowered her gaze and pretended to sniff a ladle of wine. If this theory was correct, and she had a feeling it was, then she could feel sympathy with the Carvalho family. Jacinto Douro would make an unpleasant enemy.

Leaving her thoughts, she made an effort to catch up with the conversation. Bryce was being told about the oaken pipes fashioned to mature the tawny port, and Sarah was shown an old-fashioned etching of coopers at work. Slowly they made their way towards steps at the other end of the cavern, learning how a vintage was selected and why port is drunk from a tulip-shaped glass.

Then came the hospitality room where the wine-sampling took place. Past the air-curtain, halfway up the steps could be seen a brightly lit interior lined with tiny polished barrels with wooden taps. To one side was a bar of mellowed wood holding trays of small glasses. Bryce had already gone ahead, beckoned forward by a respectful white-coated steward. Sarah was negotiating the curve of the steps in the gloom to follow when an arm came out to block her way and she heard the throaty voice of their host in her ear. "Here is the plaque that marks the doorway of the original cellar."

A glance at the pitted wall showed Sarah a metal plate, but it was too tarnished and dulled with age to read and she was sure it was not normally pointed out to visitors. She tried to push ahead and found that the arm remained to block her way. She said levelly, "If you don't mind, I'd like to get by, Senhor Douro."

"Call me Jacinto," he smiled, close to her in the shadows, his black eyes trailing her features musingly. "I like the sound of it on a lady's lips."

Viewing his dusky aquiline features and tangle of black hair Sarah could feel strongly that he had a power with women. But for her his lips were too thick and there was a shiftiness behind his smouldering gaze which she had sensed from the start. Far from being attracted by his personality her insides recoiled as he brought his hand down from the wall and brushing it against her said in caressing tones, "We have fair women in Portugal, but your hair . . . . it's like sunlight . . ."

Bryce had only been gone a few seconds, and he stepped back to see what had become of her. Taking advantage of the sight of him, Sarah pushed past Jacinto and made her way up the steps. She wasn't sure how much Bryce had seen. She had a feeling that her cheeks were slightly pink from the unpleasant encounter. Jacinto passed the whole thing off with the carefree swagger of his kind.

In the vintage room they were shown round the sampling barrels, each one displaying a date and a map of the district where the grapes had been grown. They were asked to choose their drink. Sarah had the same as Bryce, and drank without noticing the taste. Her only desire was to get out into the wholesome fresh air. Her spirits rose when they turned at last to a stairway leading to the outdoors. After a brief smile of thanks at the steward, she left Bryce voicing his appreciation for the tour and completing the farewells for them both. She arrived at the car long before he did.

As far as Sarah was concerned the nicest part about the wine lodge visit was the drive back along the street past the quaint little houses which looked as though the four or five hundred years since mediaeval times had passed them by without change. The city of Porto, spilling down the hillsides across the bridge, also looked steeped in antiquity as they approached its gothic towers and spires glinting in the pearly light which hung over the river.

The oil boss made no reference to their tour of the Douro wine cellars and Sarah had the feeling that like her he regarded the trip as merely incidental to the day. For her part she was content now to recapture their earlier mood of just ambling along, letting her gaze wander at leisure over the scenery. She liked the incredibly brilliant colours of the fishing boats in the blue water inlets they passed along the coast out of Porto. And the lush green of pines topping red sandstone cliffs of the circular bays; although she could remember a time when such scenes would have left her unmoved.

The sun was slipping into the sea, bathing everything in a golden light, as they came into the approach to Laso. The cliffs and trees and tiny boats on the water were all black cardboard cut-outs framed in fire against its brilliance. Sarah thought she must be getting over-sentimental or something, for the incredible beauty of the scene struck at her heart. She wanted to know badly how it affected Bryce, and as they were climbing the road to O Saudade she stole a glance in his direction. The rugged lines of his profile were clearly etched, yet somehow softened in the copper light. There was a look about him that made her heart swell to an even greater extent, and she had to lower her glance and pretend to be adjusting the belt of her dress as they pulled into the grounds of the house.

Her throat was too constricted to say more than a polite, "Thank you. It's been a lovely day," as Bryce gave her a hand out of the car.

A man of few words himself, he had even less to say as they stood in the last amber light of the sun. His hand momentarily holding hers, he bade her a brusque farewell, then strode away to see how the offices had fared without his presence. Sarah went quickly off to her room.

CHAPTER EIGHT

For Sarah the drive out to Porto had been a welcome change from routine. She didn't know whether Bryce Taylor was of the same opinion, but a few days later he showed signs of being dissatisfied with the work scheme as it stood. After striding about the office making a speech about developments as a whole concerning the oil refinery, he said with a brisk businesslike air, "It's not enough to open our doors to the Laso people, Miss Martindale. We must go out into the town and get to know them at first hand."

And so they locked up the office two or three afternoons a week and drove off into the sunshine. Bryce was already on familiar terms with the tradespeople in Laso. He still had his rooms at the hotel and it was obvious that he had spent much of his spare time in improving the image of Pyramid Oil in the vicinity. There was no doubt that he was popular with the locals.

But there was a strong element of opposition in some parts of the town. It was Sarah's job to help him break down the barriers of reserve where they existed and to further the oil company's good name by making amends where they could for the imposition of their presence. It was not difficult to get to know the wants of a community as small as Laso and in the hot sunshine the oil boss, casually dressed in light slacks and open-necked shirt, and Sarah in cool summer dress, were a familiar sight strolling amongst the colourful Portuguese inhabitants and making friends with the local authorities. And there seemed to be no limit to what Pyramid Oil were prepared to do to get their way.

On behalf of the oil company Bryce Taylor sponsored a new wing for the local library. His offer to restore the historic buildings surrounding the garden centre of the town was accepted after some consideration. One afternoon Sarah accompanied him to the school and there was talk of a new extension to the dining section. As Bryce strolled and talked and smiled and listened, Sarah was there strolling too, and ready when he gave the word, as he frequently did, "Make a note of that Miss Martindale."

Wherever they went in the town the oil boss's policy was to make it known that anyone who might be displaced by the plans for the oil refinery would be amply compensated.

They made many friends on these afternoon jaunts, and just as they had been invited to the wine lodge at Porto, they were invited into the Laso people's homes. Sarah sat and sipped wine in cool stone-floored interiors and listened to the local gossip under grape trellises facing the sea.

Much of the conversation on these occasions was lost on her, for the people who had to earn their living from the sea spoke their own language. And though Sarah was becoming familiar with the strange sounds she hadn't yet reached the point where she could make much out of it. Bryce Taylor, on the other hand, was perfectly at home chatting in either language. Sarah had heard talk among the technicians that he had worked for the oil company in Brazil and had been picked for the Laso job because of his knowledge of Portuguese. Whatever the case he certainly spoke it well. All Sarah could do was smile and let the gossip pass over her head.

But what did she care about talk? Whether they were in a fisherman's cottage where she didn't understand a word, or the garden of a businessman's villa where immaculate English was spoken, it was all the same to her. She had the satin-smooth apron of sea studded with brilliantly coloured craft to look at, and a sky bluer than the colour in a painter's palette. The air was fragrant with pine and eucalyptus and trailing wistaria. The sun shone warmly, and Bryce was constantly by her side.

On those long summer afternoons Sarah fell in love with Portugal; with its fierce colours and friendly people; and with life. She couldn't think now what she had ever found to admire in the musty, dickensian atmosphere of the marine lawyer's offices in Southampton. Her life of those days was no more than a dim and distant memory. One she had no wish to recall. Here, gazing at a view alongside Bryce, walking with him in town amidst the crowded pavement café tables, or climbing a pebbly slope to some elegant household, her heart sang in a way that it had never sung before. And then one afternoon her rainbow world disintegrated.

They never had much occasion to visit the harbour-side with its warehouses and offices, but Bryce wanted to pick up some important papers and they drove there after a pleasant interlude sipping *vinho verde* with the town secretary. As they cruised up the hill past the crescent of beach and on to park along the harbour front Sarah was stunned by the changes that had been made. In her rosy world of the past weeks she hadn't paid much attention to the progress charts in the oil offices at O Saudade, but it was clear to see that Pyramid Oil had taken a great step forward. Gone were all the little harbour-side concerns of the past and everywhere along the wharfside there was evidence of the all-powerful oil company.

As though to confirm her fears the oil boss strode out from the company offices to where she was standing gazing at the scene beside the car and tapped the papers in his hand with a satisfied gleam. "This ties up the list of the harbour-side properties." He put the papers in his briefcase, tossed it into the car, then dropping an arm lightly across Sarah's shoulder he pointed along the wharfside. "As far as you can see is Pyramid Oil," he said vibrantly. "The wine-shipping firm at the end won't sell, but we needn't let them stand in our way."

Sarah watched the Carvalhos' wine tankers being loaded and felt the ground sway beneath her feet. Bryce must have noticed her drained features, for he asked, watching her. "What's wrong? Doesn't the good news please you?"

"Oh yes, I think it's wonderful," Sarah made an effort to sound enthusiastic. She tried to pass off her queasy look with a light-hearted, "Too much wine. They say that *vinho verde* is heady if you don't watch it, and I'm beginning to think it's true." She prattled on about nothing at all, pretending to crinkle her eyes at the view and the bobbing fishing boats and feeling all the time that Bryce was watching her sharply. Luckily as he helped her into the car she caught her foot on a mooring ring and stumbled badly. She hoped it really did look as though the wine was to blame for her odd behaviour.

It was no surprise to Sarah to receive a summons a few days later to the Carvalhos' *quinta*. On a free afternoon she had gone down into Laso with the Valadins to do some necessary personal shopping. Januario, the Carvalhos' chauffeur, approached her in a crowded street in the same manner as last time. Without a word she went with him to the car in a side alley from where she was driven out speedily to the Quinta.

Senhor Carvalho was not on the steps of the house to greet her. He was pacing in his office when she was shown in. Though he greeted her in his usual courteous manner, it was clear he was concerned at the headway being made by Pyramid Oil. He studied the map and questioned Sarah. Like her, he was shocked at the hold the oil company had obtained at the harbour.

"Lamentably, the fishermen don't need the wharfside," he said, frowning. "They can beach their boats anywhere on the stretch of sand." He considered the points before him on the map, then tapped the region of the oil refinery site, the vast tracts of land that Sarah had seen on the other side of town. "This is where the oil man is going to spread his energies next." As there were already several shaded areas here Senhor Carvalho added heavily, "From now on, Miss Martindale, I must ask you to make a weekly report."

On the ride back to town Sarah too experienced a minor feeling of panic at the way things were going. She had never expected the oil boss to come so far in achieving his aims. The chances of his succeeding had looked so gloomy at the start that she had considered it only a question of time before the oil refinery plan in Laso had to be dropped. Yet here he was demolishing the opposition with his rugged charm, and moving steadily ahead.

She had been deceived into a false calm. She had seen him show pleasure in the little things like viewing O Saudade for the first time, and choosing the bric-a-brac for the rooms, not knowing that in business he was as ruthless as the next man when there was something he wanted.

If she had known he was going to get this far nothing would have induced her to take the job for the Carvalhos. But she had done and now there was no way out. She could only hope that there would be insurmountable obstacles ahead for Pyramid Oil.

The next few days were trying ones for Sarah. She made an effort to hide the strain she was feeling by putting on a bright air around the oil offices, but often she sensed the oil boss watching her thoughtfully. When they went into town she was a bundle of nerves, terrified that the Carvalhos' chauffeur would accost her when she was thus accompanied. She ought to have known that the wine family were much too discreet for that. But as she had no specific arrangements to go by concerning her visits to the *quinta* she never knew when the dreaded moment was about to be thrust on her.

On one particular occasion she was certain the call had no better. She went about her tasks furtively, posting mail and completing oil company business, with the constant feeling that someone was going to tap her on the shoulder at any second.

On one particular occasion she was certain the call had come, though she thought Januario was being over-familiar when an arm curved around her waist and a voice said throatily in her ear, "*Boa tarde*, Senhorita Martindale. Can I give you a lift somewhere?"

She swung round jumpily and met the dark sensual gaze of Jacinto Douro. How many times she had looked into those eyes just lately. Ever since her visit to the wine cellar with Bryce Jacinto had been a regular visitor to O Saudade. As a man in favour of the oil refinery he was a valuable ally to Pyramid Oil and was invited to all the oil company receptions. Sarah could put up with his company on the cocktail party afternoons when the guests wandered over the lawns and she could keep him at a distance. But in the evenings, when he would let his lips linger over-long on her hand in greeting, she found his presence unbearable. As subtly as she could she made it clear that she detested him, but this only seemed to kindle the fire in his eyes.

Tugging away from him now, she saw as she turned that he was standing beside an expensive racy type of sports car, a brilliant apple green in colour. They were in a side street with shady awnings and bowls of flowers in the shop doorways. The car almost blocked the way with its opulent width, and it struck Sarah as being a rather luxurious item for Jacinto to possess. From what she had seen of the family wine business she wouldn't have thought he made enough to indulge in such extravagant tastes.

Showing no signs of being impressed as he swayed before her in his tight black trousers and vivid green shirt, she said acidly, "I have all the transport I need, thank you. And if I hadn't I'd find walking infinitely more acceptable than riding with you."

Jacinto's black eyes smouldered satirically. "So, the cool white English rose has thorns." He conjectured, smiling over her, "We must find a way to clip them."

"Please go away, and take your toys with you, Senhor Douro," Sarah gave him a cutting smile. "I have work to do."

For a moment as he stood blocking her path she saw his saturnine features darken stormily and the smile on his face curl into one of suppressed rage. Then he climbed into his car, opened the throttle noisily and thundered away along the street and out of sight.

Sarah watched him go with a slightly worried look. Though it had given her considerable satisfaction to put him in his place, her instinct told her that he was a dangerous man to snub.

As the days grew hotter and the sun sparkled down on the sea, entertaining at O Saudade graduated towards the beach. Most of the people of Laso owned boats and often the water bordering the strip of sand would be dotted with all kinds of picturesque little craft. The more important guests always arrived in spanking white speedboats or elegant yachts and together with the oil company staff who had all hired vessels of some kind there was often quite a gathering.

Informality was the rule on these occasions. There were picnics from tablecloths on the rocks and Eduardo, looking slightly incongruous in black coat and pin-striped trousers, served at a bar beneath a gay awning beside the steps. For the oil staff it was a semi-holiday, as they revelled in the beauty of the private strip of beach where the water was now a flat limpid blue with barely the whisper of a wave to fall on the bleached white sand, and the tree-clad slopes behind, spangled with wild flowers, were vividly picked out against the blue of the sky.

There were tanned bodies everywhere. Sarah in cool sun-dress would pass sandwiches around or carry a tray of drinks to where they were needed. Good-naturedly Bryce made himself useful in a similar way. He wore bright sailcloth slacks and coloured shirts that made his rugged features look darkly tanned. Sometimes when Sarah looked at him her heart would turn a somersault.

They often attended to the same group together. He

must have seen her signature on office literature, but not knowing much about feminine names he called her Sara with a flat *a* sound, in a way which rhymed with tiara. Sarah didn't dislike it.

Of course, Jacinto Douro was always there somewhere in the background. Though he had passed her by in town on several occasions in his racy sports car, pausing to bow to her satirically over the wheel, he had never approached her since the day she had cut him dead. But at the beach he flaunted his powered craft in front of her whenever he could, and made a point of strolling at close quarters in his tailored white swim shorts which flattered his olive-skinned sinewy frame.

Sarah took little notice of him. She was far too occupied listening to the distant music playing in her heart. On days like these, stumbling smilingly through the sand, meeting Bryce's sea-green gaze now and then, she was inclined to forget everything, even her worries concerning the oil refinery.

But it was never for long. There were always her trips to the Carvalhos' *quinta*—she was now making regular weekly visits—to remind her that Pyramid Oil was breathing over her shoulder. And the news she had to report on these occasions only served to increase Senhor Carvalho's concern.

A sign that the oil company were growing increasingly optimistic came one day when news was received in the offices of an important visit to be made by company lawyers, administrators, and various other V.I.P.s of Pyramid Oil. It was Sarah's job to organise a grand reception at O Saudade in their honour and of course to include as many big names in Laso as possible.

The house was a hive of activity in preparation for the visit. The gardens and grounds were given a new face-lift by hired gardeners, and the rooms received special attention. There were no problems with accommodation, thank heaven, for the men would be flying into Porto, then flying out again. The Valadins were delighted at the news. Preparing picnic fare was a little beneath their dignity. Now at last they could fill the buffet tables with the type of splendid cuisine they were noted for and so regain a little of their prestige. To give a Portuguese flavour to the scene, a group of local musicians was hired to take the place of the taped music.

On the night of the event Sarah was weak with apprehension. She had so much to hide these days, and so much to feel a bitter-sweet ache inside for. She put on for the first time the white gown with the flowing lines and gold encircling throat piece, feeling that she was at last up to its regal look. Her arms and V-shaped portion of bare shoulder had the dusting of a peach-coloured tan. Pale with strain under the soft bloom of summer on her cheeks, she had twisted her hair, now grown long, into a knot which rested on the nape of her neck. This gave her profile something of a fragile look.

She was downstairs and waiting when the fleet of black cars made its way up towards the lights of the house and parked in the grounds. Bryce Taylor, tall and spruce in dark dinner jacket and trousers, went out to meet them, but Sarah stayed in her place in the hall until they arrived.

A group of hearty grey-haired men who laughed a lot, and who wore their Savile Row suits with the careless detachment that goes with success, they shook Sarah's hand warmly and beamed approval at all they saw. As the reception got under way they mingled with the guests, not without ulterior motive, of course, though their amiable faces and casual manner gave the impression that business was the farthest thing from their minds.

The rooms were tastefully lit, and the trees in the grounds were strung with fairy lights. Everybody—for there seemed to be half of Laso here tonight—wandered in and out into the summer evening at their leisure. In the main lounge, the Portuguese musicians, colourfully dressed in red waistcoats, black trousers and green hats, produced a constant flow of lively tunes on their dais in the walk-in fireplace.

Sarah was kept busy checking the food at the buffet tables, keeping a watch on the drink stock and generally making sure that things were running smooth. She toured the rooms, aware of the glances she attracted as she moved. She was just a little rapturous that Bryce's gaze hardly ever left her as she passed in and out of the main lounge.

She saw Jacinto Douro on several occasions. His sensually brooding glance, following her, was like a blow sometimes when she met it. But she had no trouble ignoring him. Her mind was on far loftier planes tonight.

Of course there came a time during the evening when she had to give her attention solely to the oil company officials. They expected her to have a drink with them and this she did, smiling at their remarks and listening with a sympathetic ear as they told her stories of their spouses, and children, and children's children.

They were obviously pleased at the way things were going in Laso and made no effort to hide it. Howard Mason, the company's chief attorney, a big man with a deep infectious laugh and a rascally blue gaze, toasted Sarah with his glass and said above the din in the room, "No doubt you have your lovely assistant to thank for much of your success in the town, Bryce?"

Sarah felt herself blush at the compliment. The oil boss took a drink from his glass and swallowed with his lopsided smile. No one waited for him to reply, for all the men's attention was focussed on Sarah. She had to suffer several more flattering remarks before she excused herself to have a word with Eduardo about supper for the musicians.

Later she viewed Bryce from afar, surrounded by his senior colleagues. She watched him talking in relaxed pose and the bitter-sweet ache inside her turned into a stab of pain. What was it all for? The noise, the gaiety, the bright lights, the party atmosphere? There might have been a feeling of success in the air for Pyramid Oil, but Sarah knew different. The oil boss was never going to get his oil refinery in Laso. She knew it and there was nothing she could do about it. If she told him now about the harbour deeds, he would have to know that she had been working as a spy for the Carvalhos all these months. And that was something she couldn't bear for him to find out.

A brilliance in her gaze as she watched his smile, lazily confident, she swung quickly away and turned to other things.

The oil company officials took their leave around midnight. They shook Bryce genially by the hand and included Sarah in their last-minute salutes. "Keep up the good work, Miss Martindale." Then they were driven away, back towards Porto and their private jet.

The Laso guests were more reluctant to tear themselves away, and it was almost two before the last of them departed. The hired staff went quickly into action clearing up after the evening. Sarah, longing for a quiet moment, drifted out through a side door to the loggia whose leafy roof showed a sprinkling of stars through the tangled gaps. There was peace here and a lingering perfume from nearby roses. If she listened she could hear the distant sigh of the sea on the beach down below.

Gradually her tension lessened. She felt soothed by the rustling of the breeze. She was listening to a night bird picking up a call from afar when a footstep behind startled her. It was dark, but she could tell by the bulk of the frame that it was Bryce. She had been under the impression that he had left for Laso and his hotel some time ago.

She thought he had come to comment on the evening as he sometimes did before leaving. She waited. He said, after a long moment, "Quite a night!"

"Yes, wasn't it?" Sarah replied, trying to sound offhand.

"The big brass were quite impressed by my personal assistant."

Sarah made no comment to this vibrant offering. The sound of the sea came up to fall on the silence between them. Bryce tapped his pipe on anything he could find, a habit he had when he was a little ill at ease.

Sarah stood in the darkness feeling her tension rising again. She stammered, "It's a little late . . . I . . ."

As she turned, Bryce thrust his pipe into his jacket pocket and caught her close to him. Locked in his arms, Sarah received his lips with a hunger she never knew she possessed. With a similar hunger he strained her against him. Afire with the ecstasy of his touch, she let him drain her lips, caring nothing for the taint of deceit which dogged her. Only when it made itself known to her, when she saw herself clinging to him, knowing what she was doing to him, did she pull away.

Steadying herself, patting her hair with trembling hands, she said in shattered tones, "I wish you hadn't done that."

"Do you?" He looked at her, a glimmer of embarrassment in his crooked smile as he straightened his tie. Did he know something of her true feelings? She couldn't have said. As her bosom rose and fell he turned in the darkness and disappeared. A few seconds later she heard his car start up and move out of the grounds, heading for town.

CHAPTER NINE

AFTER the visit of the oil officials, work in the company offices at O Saudade accelerated. Bryce Taylor transferred his energies to the reluctant landowners still clinging to their properties at the refinery site. He spent long hours in negotiations around the district. This gave him very little time for office work.

Sarah was relieved in a way that he was out such a lot. She couldn't look him in the eye these days, and after their turbulent embrace in the loggia that night, it was doubly difficult trying to keep a composed look. But in another way she was terrified when she thought of the ground he might be gaining while he was out on these expeditions. With his persuasive talk and powerful oil company backing she never knew who was going to capitulate next to Pyramid Oil. One thing she could be certain of. The news was always grim on her visits to the Carvalhos' *quinta*. Senhor Carvalho viewed each report with a gloom akin to Sarah's.

Though she hated the trips she could see no way out of the growing nightmare. Her one hope was that Bryce would come up against a supreme obstacle which would put paid once and for all to the idea of an oil refinery in Laso.

She detested, too, her clandestine meetings with the Carvalhos' chauffeur. She never knew from week to week which spot he would choose in town to drift up close to her, under cover of the local bustle. She knew this was done to protect her as well as the Carvalhos. Nevertheless it was nerve-racking, to say the least, wandering around, pretending to be leisurely shopping, and all the time waiting for that ominous tap on the shoulder.

On one of these tense afternoons something happened which only served to increase her nervous state. Under something of a strain as she always was on the *quinta* afternoons, she had walked with Januario round the corner from the main line of shops in the square, where he had approached her, to the sleek black family car parked in a side alley.

It was when they were pulling quietly away that Sarah thought she caught a glimpse of an apple green sports car in the rear view mirror. That was all it had been, a glimpse as they cruised away from the traffic in the square, but it was enough to start Sarah's heart thumping erratically. She looked quickly back as they slid along the side alley. There was nothing. A flood of relief washed over her. She relaxed sufficiently to sit back on their route through town and on to the twisting, climbing Amorida valley road.

But her nerves were on edge. Several times during the drive she thought she sensed a presence behind them. Imagination, of course. But was it? As they sped towards the Carvalho estate along the lonely road she was racked by a feeling of doubt. Each time she turned to fling a nervous glance out of the rear window the road was empty. And yet it seemed to her that above the steady hum of the engine another, a thundering, racing type, echoed faintly in the distance on the road behind them.

She found her interview with Senhor Carvalho more trying than usual. He was ruthless with his questions concerning the latest developments in the oil offices, and Sarah knew better than to try and paint an optimistic picture when everything was going so well for Pyramid Oil. The wine-grower, however, had a spot of bright news to offer.

He tapped the map on his desk and told Sarah, "These vast tracts of land to the west of the oil refinery site are owned by two of the oldest families in Portugal. The Ribieros are descended from the nobility in Porto and have powerful connections in the city. The Serveras, residing in Estoril, can trace their ancestry back to the old empire-building days. Both are known to be rigorously nationalistic and in favour of boycotting foreign investments." Senhor Carvalho gave a little musing smile. "They should, between them, I think, provide some formidable opposition for our oil man."

Sarah hoped that he was right. She took her leave at the end of the afternoon, exhausted as usual with the unsavoury business of intrigue. She kept a sharp eye open on the drive back to town. The country road was deserted. The only travellers they passed from time to time were the drivers of the farm bullock carts and donkey-drawn conveyances. Sarah breathed easier. It must have been her imagination after all.

Although Bryce Taylor had charmed his way into the hearts of the Laso people, Pyramid Oil still had an image to keep in the town and evening receptions became the practice as autumn approached. Sarah knew there was one planned for the week-end following her visit to the Carvalhos, and she was dreading it. There was no escaping the probing gaze of the oil boss on these occasions, for no matter where his negotiations took him through the day, he always made a point of being at Sarah's side in the evening to welcome the guests to O Saudade.

She prepared for the evening half hoping to find when she got downstairs that he had been held up somewhere out of town, for she was sure she would never pass his stringent contemplation of her without giving something away. She slipped into a peacock blue gown, which unfortunately gave her features an alabaster paleness. But there was no time to have second thoughts on the matter. Downstairs, things were already livening up. Quickly she went out and took the stairs. As she did so she saw with that familiar twist at her heart that Bryce was back. Big and tanned in dark lounge suit, he was already in his place at the door.

As she came down the curving staircase he did something he had never done before—he turned and watched her progress. Sarah's hand trembled as she clutched the rail. Perhaps it was just his way of acknowledging her before the commencement of their duties as hosts. Or perhaps his keen eye detected the feeling of guilt which engulfed her. Her nerves were so frayed as her mind gnawed at first one possibility and then another, it was all she could do to keep her composure. She moved down and took her place before him, directing her tense smile towards the outdoors.

As soon as the flow of cars finished and the guests were wandering at leisure through the rooms of the house Sarah hurried away. No one knew better than her that there was little to attend to at a small reception such as this. The buffet tables were piled high with the Valadins' specialities, castles and mountains of piquant concoctions, and the white-coated stewards were unlikely to run out of wine for their trays. But she needed an excuse to look busy to keep herself from falling apart.

Two coins of colour showed on her cheeks when she thought of all she was trying to hide, though her finger tips were like ice. She was making a pretence of arranging the curtains at the casement window in one of the smaller smoking rooms when a hand touched her arm and trailed slowly over her skin. In her ear a voice drawled ironically, "Good evening, O cool rose of England."

Sarah jumped round. Her flesh creeping, she must have known it was the swarthy Jacinto's touch. Or had it been more of a caress? Trembling with nerves but trying not to show it, she said in the acid tones she reserved for the oily Portuguese, "Kindly get out of my way, Senhor Douro. I have things to do."

"Oh, come now!" Jacinto's smile showed his nicotine-stained teeth. "That's no way to talk to an *old* friend."

Closer to him than she cared to be, Sarah searched his shadowy aquiline features. He was certainly acting very strangely tonight. And there were tiny pin-points of flame in his bold black gaze roaming over her, which started her pulses thumping apprehensively.

Taking advantage of the appearance of a laughing middle-aged foursome, she pushed past Jacinto as though he were part of the furniture. But though she went on her way haughtily she felt his eyes watching her go with a musingly undeterred gleam.

She found the crowded lounge infinitely more preferable after the unpleasant interlude. But here more demands were made on her. She was drawn into conversation with groups who were now more like old friends than guests, and people at the buffet tables wanted her to join them in a drink. And then there was Bryce, himself busily engaged with a party, but not too busy, Sarah noticed, to follow her with his green gaze from time to time.

Her main occupation was in keeping a calm exterior. This she managed to do, though her smiling features were merely a veneer to hide the havoc going on inside her. There was a limit to how long she could keep up the pretence of gaiety, however, and to gain a little respite from the laughing guests she slipped away for a few moments.

There was a room adjoining the main lounge which had been furnished as a kind of study. Flanking the alcove window and writing desk were twin bookshelves and in the centre of the room was a red settee and low wood coffee table. Sarah liked to come here for a few moments' peace on a hectic night. The sounds of the house were shut out, and there was the soothing tick-tock of a figured china clock on the mantelshelf.

She slipped inside now, screened by a talkative group, and closed the door quietly behind her. It was heaven to breathe in the smoke-free air and to feel its cool freshness on her burning cheeks. She was too keyed up to sit down, but just wandering alone in the peace helped a lot. She was fingering a copper flower vase absently on a small wall-side table when she heard the door open softly and close quietly again. As she wheeled round, her startled gaze met the saturnine Jacinto's.

Her first reaction was one of annoyance. But something about his smiling self-assured attitude, coupled with the memory of his peculiar behaviour earlier on in the evening, started up a little warning signal in her brain. She said nothing as he swaggered into the room. He said, mimicking the English idiom as he looked around, "Well now! Isn't this cosy!"

Unable to bear his strutting self-conceit, Sarah snapped, "What do you want?"

Jacinto examined items around the room in a maddeningly idle fashion. Shooting Sarah a barely concealed calculating glint, he asked playfully, "Do you really want to know?"

His usually immaculate English was thickened tonight by a strong Portuguese accent, brought on, Sarah felt sure, by some inner excitement he was trying hard to contain. Because she didn't reply he continued to cruise about the room. Then choosing his own moment he asked, weighing his words carefully, "You find our Amorida valley pretty at this time of the year, do you not?"

Sarah felt the colour drain from her face, but she tried to sound unaffected as she suggested witheringly, "Wouldn't it save a lot of time if you were to come straight out with what you have to say?"

"But who's short of time?" Jacinto raised his black eyebrows innocently. "I'm not. And you certainly aren't." Tauntingly he lit up a cigarette with an expensive lighter, then blowing out the smoke he gleamed at her. "You can afford to take long rides in the country every week."

Sarah's knees buckled. She had to clutch at the back of the settee for support. "So it *was* your car I saw in town that day," she said faintly, half to herself. And knowing now that she was lost, "You followed us."

"Far enough to know where you were going," Jacinto smiled smoothly. "I spotted you in the square in Laso and watched your shady little rendezvous with the Carvalho chauffeur with interest." He strolled around, musing over her at leisure as he drew on his cigarette. "I wonder what the oil man would think if he knew his trusty assistant was working for the other side?"

"You wouldn't dare tell him!" White-faced, Sarah swayed forward.

Jacinto let his gaze roam over her and said with his flame-lit gleam, "I might be persuaded to hold my tongue. Or to put it another way, shall we say . . . I have a price?"

Sarah felt her cheeks blaze. Behind her shattered exterior her mind was racing. He must have done more than follow the Carvalhos' car to know all he seemed to know. Eyeing him with distaste, she asked, "How did you find out . . . about me?"

"It was quite simple," Jacinto gave her his innocuous smile. "Januario Ferreira has a brother who works in a winery under Douro supervision in Vila Nova de Gaia. He has five children and an invalid wife to support." Jacinto paused for effect before adding with an odious gleam, "I merely told Januario that his brother could find himself without a job if he didn't tell me the reason for your visits to the *quinta*."

"You're despicable!" Sarah spat the words at him.

"You think that now," Jacinto moved in close to her with his taunting gleam. "You'll change your mind when you get to know me better."

"I've never found vermin attractive," Sarah flung at him.

"No!" With a flash of anger in his eyes Jacinto caught her close in a grip that almost snapped her in two. "But you'll play along with me, I think," he smiled over her. "It wouldn't do for Taylor to get wind of your meetings with the Carvalhos, would it?"

Knowing that she had no choice but to do as he said, Sarah remained wooden in his embrace. She shuddered as he trailed his thick sensual lips lingeringly over her throat, but when he brought them down, slightly parted, on to hers, she broke free with a sob of revulsion and stumbled towards the door.

Jacinto laughed softly as she tried to scrape together enough composure to step out into the crowded lounge. The last thing she saw as she turned out of the room was his triumphant smile.

It was lucky that the reception was going with a swing, for everyone was far too occupied to notice Sarah's white face as she merged into the gathering. It was only by chance that she met Bryce Taylor's glance. Though he was invariably engaged in conversation, wherever he was in the room his green gaze would always search her out. Immediately she knew he had seen her leave the small study.

Jacinto came out after her. Unlike her, he had no idea they were being watched. On trembling legs Sarah tried to find something to do. A heaven-sent escape came in the form of a guest, a culinary expert who, dazzled by the Valadins' succulent displays, insisted on knowing more about them. Willingly Sarah took the woman along to the kitchen, though how she managed to propel her swaying self along under the oil boss's stringent gaze she never knew.

She took advantage of the opportunity to hide away amongst the pots and pans for the short time there was left of the evening. The Valadins and the food enthusiast, rattling away together in Portuguese, paid little attention to her as she pretended to supervise the stewards hurrying in and out with their trays, and to check ostensibly the contents of the *hors d'oeuvres* and reserve platters of salad.

She made a brief appearance in the main lounge as the guests started to leave, waiting only long enough for the cars to start rumbling off on their way back to town before she fled to her room.

She didn't go immediately to bed. Still in her gown, she paced, staggered by the events of the evening and racked with worry. Jacinto knew she was working for the Carvalhos. Her heart thudded with alarm at this new danger. He was prepared to stay silent on one condition. She shuddered with disgust as she recalled his passionate embrace. And yet a far deeper dread which dogged her was the horror of Bryce Taylor discovering her deceit.

How could she bear it if he ever found out she had been working against him all these months; that she had known from the start that he would never succeed in launching an oil refinery in Laso? She wrung her hands at the grim aspect. Even Jacinto didn't know about the ancient harbour deeds in the Carvalhos' possession. That was a terrible knowledge that Sarah had to carry alone.

It was the early hours before she slumped down on the bed, having decided on the course she would take. Senhor Carvalho had talked of powerful opposition which could put an end to the idea of an oil refinery in Laso. If this happened Bryce need never know about her work for the wine family or the harbour deeds. She closed her eyes at last, limp with exhaustion. To keep her secret she knew she would do anything Jacinto asked.

After that disastrous evening Sarah spent her time close to O Saudade. She gave the letters for posting to one of the technicians and made excuses to the Valadins for not joining them on the car trips into town. As far as was possible she made a pretence of being busy with oil company matters.

For one or two hours a day Bryce caught up with the work on his desk. Ever since that night on the loggia the reserve had thickened between them, though Sarah had the feeling that he watched her all the time.

Her one hope as she went tremblingly about her tasks was that he would keep the house free of guests. But that was too much to ask. The only way he could wear his opponents down was to invite them to O Saudade and wine them and dine them, before working towards his aims. And the Ribieros, the landowners connected with nobility, whom Senhor Carvalho had mentioned, were no excpetion to this rule. Their names were at the top of a list of invitations he made out for a reception to be held in a few days' time. It was Sarah's job to send out the invitations. As she had feared, Jacinto Douro's name was there amongst the list of guests.

How she dragged through the hours until the night of the reception she never knew. She went about her duties mechanically, planning the evening, making sure that all would run smooth, with one thought gnawing at her insides. *Jacinto.*

She toyed with the idea of being missing on the night, but that would only attract suspicion to herself, and heaven knew she had to tread carefully as it was. The oil boss seemed to miss nothing these days. No, there was nothing to be done but to get through the evening somehow.

When the time came she showered as usual and used the perfume from Casimiro's lavishly. She daren't do anything but look her best. On the face of it she had to do all she could to win the Ribieros over to Pyramid Oil. She dragged herself around in a fog of despair. What a position to be in! She had no choice but to work towards the very thing that spelled disaster—victory for Bryce Taylor.

She chose a gown of green chiffon with a spangled bodice, and dressed her hair, entwining a cord of gold in its silken coil. She made up carefully, endeavouring to disguise the shadows of strain under her eyes and the distraught look which she couldn't seem to shake off. The Ribieros were very important guests, so there was no question of not being down at the door to meet them. But like all prominent people they took their time in showing up. Sarah had to stand in the doorway apparently cool and composed beside Bryce, waiting for their arrival and making small talk with the other guests who were drifting in.

Her pulses pounded in her head when she saw Jacinto approaching along the lamplit path together with several others. He was wearing a black suit tonight with a frilled white front and a narrow looped black tie. Though he might have been considered attractive in a swarthy fashion, only Sarah knew the depths he was prepared to stoop to to get his way.

She knew the message behind the smouldering sardonic gleam he gave her and tried hard to ignore it as he kissed her hand lingeringly. She was terrified Bryce would suspect something in his manner and worked hard at hiding her pallor behind a smile, knowing that the hooded green gaze was fixed on her. Jacinto drifted off, but she felt his odious presence in the room somewhere behind and knew that he was merely biding his time until she had to go in and mingle with the guests.

She worked herself up to such a state at the thought of that moment that when the Ribieros arrived she was hardly aware of their glittering presence. She supposed she must have smiled and said all the right things, but her recollections of the couple, an elderly pair wearing an air of breeding, were hazy. It seemed to her, as she fought to keep a picture of calm, that she had stepped outside of herself and was watching the sparkle and gaiety of the evening without taking any part in it.

Leaving the Ribieros in the capable hands, to say nothing of the persuasive charm, of Bryce Taylor, she drifted around through the blur of people, talking and smiling over an inner tension which was a drain on her strength.

She saw Jacinto several times. Though his eyes, luminescent and taunting, never left her, he made no attempt to approach her. She realised with a mixture of loathing and despair that he was enjoying playing the cat and mouse game with her.

Once he took a glass from the tray she was handing around and touched it to his lips in a way that she was not meant to miss. Another time he stood almost blocking her path so that she had to brush close to him to get by. How she hated his insinuating gestures! But the evening was passing on. In another hour she would be able to escape to her room having completed her duties for the day.

She began to feel safe. She would ignore Jacinto. Perhaps his talk had been nothing but bluff anyway. Her spirits lightened microscopically. She threw herself into the business of playing the perfect hostess. She had a feeling she over-acted a little; that there was just a fraction too much vivacity in her manner, a slightly pasted-on look about her smile. The oil boss was watching her, but she didn't care. The all-important thing was to forget the repugnant Jacinto, and this she found she could do very easily weaving amongst the laughing guests.

It was almost eleven-thirty. Soon now the people would start to leave. In her over-wrought state Sarah had almost forgotten about the Ribieros. But it wasn't for her to try and sell them the idea of the oil refinery, thank heavens. All she had to do was keep the reception wheels well oiled, and a few more minutes . . .

With shaking hands she was removing a tray of empty glasses from a small wall-side table when she turned, to find Eduardo almost behind her. "Excuse me, madam," he said in his discreet tones. "Senhor Douro asked me to give you this."

At the sight of the small folded sheet of paper on the silver tray Sarah's gaze widened in alarm. She lowered the tray of glasses and took the slip trying to appear composed as she replied waveringly, "Thank you, Eduardo."

A quick glance at the note made the room spin before her momentarily as she read the words, *Meet me on the beach in five minutes*. She felt her face go chalk white. She badly wanted to steady herself, but she had to remember she was being watched. Bryce was standing over by the fireplace and she knew his glance was raking her.

Crumpling the note in her hand, she picked up the tray of glasses again, trying hard to steady their rattle, and made her way as erectly and as naturally as she could out of the room. Once she had deposited the tray in the kitchen she found it impossible to stave off the cold panic that gripped her. Jacinto was waiting for her. He had grown tired of playing his games. She knew now that the swaggering Portuguese was deadly serious. If she didn't go to him he would waste no time in telling the oil boss everything.

The thought wrenched her heart, but she gathered her shattered self together and started on her way. She dared not disobey.

The smaller rooms were emptying. Sarah chose the one adjoining the courtyard and slipped out quietly into the night. After the brightness of the house, the outdoors took a little getting used to. Under a black sky faintly scattered with stars she picked her way through the pots and shrubbery in the courtyard and eventually out into the grounds.

The warmth of summer was still in the air, but the guests were gathered within the cheery brilliance indoors. Sarah shivered as she stumbled along the paths towards the cliff steps. She could hear the steady thresh of the waves down below above the rustling swish of her gown as she moved.

The house, a haven of laughter and noise, receded. Facing her was a lonely world of drifting clouds, and night cries and breeze-rustling undergrowth. The insidious perfume of eucalyptus came to her as she descended. Her heart thudding, her feet feeling the way tremulously, it was all she could do to keep her balance on the steep way down.

The sharp sea breezes met her. They moulded her dress to her form. She could see the pale strip of sand and the white-edged tumbling waves stretching far out into the night as she came down.

Her light shoes touched the sand. She stood, not knowing which way to go. Then that sardonic voice that she knew so well came to her from the shadows at the side. "So our cool white English rose prefers to keep an untarnished image with her employer?"

How Sarah loathed his taunting humour! She said,

mechanically, a chill brushing her skin at his nearness, making her voice shake, "I got your note, and I came as you asked."

"As we both knew you would," Jacinto said silkily, smiling at her out of the darkness. His black eyes glowed by the light of the stars. His tone was thickly accented as he drew her towards him. "I wanted to tell you earlier—you're looking beautiful tonight."

Sarah caught a whiff of his breath, sour with too much wine, and a wave of faintness engulfed her. He was pressing her close. Those thick sensual lips were searching for hers. She couldn't turn away, but the moment his mouth descended upon hers she knew she must.

Nauseated beyond endurance, she pushed against him frantically. His grip was like steel, and he seemed lost to her struggles. She could feel the rough grass and undergrowth of the rockery at her back as she fought to rid herself of his lips.

His hands were roaming her body. A sob was locked in her throat. She twisted and writhed, then all at once she fell free. The bodice of her dress flapped at her shoulder and Jacinto, stumbling back or overbalancing as it gave way—Sarah didn't wait to see which—was for one brief second just a blot in the darkness.

That second was long enough for her to make a lunge towards the steps. Mercifully she found the first one and gathering her dress up for speed half fell up the winding route. But the going was steep, and Jacinto was already on her trail. She heard his soft exhilarated laugh behind her.

Her legs felt like lead weights as she tried to keep them going. Frantically she scrabbled on. The effort of running and climbing ever upwards made her lungs feel as though they were bursting. She could hear Jacinto scrambling up close behind her. He was breathless too with the climb, but his gasps were more of exultation compared with Sarah's agonised sobs.

Several times she almost fell. Her legs were beginning to give way beneath her. She reeled on, but the dark sky was spinning around her. Half-way up the path she clutched and fell gasping on to one of the tiled look-out seats. Jacinto was just an arm's length away, but racked with shortage of breath Sarah knew she couldn't go on.

She felt his warm hand turn round her wrist to pull her to him, then a voice ripped through the darkness, making them both start. "Senhor Douro!"

Sarah, heaving painfully, stared towards the steps, and was horror-stricken to see the dark shape of Bryce Taylor standing there. Silhouetted against the pale skyline, his profile seemed etched in steel. His eyes reflecting the meagre light from the stars were like molten flame. He continued, in that deceptively calm tone which was like an icy wind slicing towards Jacinto, "I trust that whatever business you have with my personal assistant can be explained?"

Sarah, holding her torn dress to her shoulder, felt her heart thudding under her hand. She heard Jacinto, close to her, say with arrogant amusement, "These things are a little delicate to put into words, Senhor Taylor. But ask your assistant." Sarah knew he was wielding his power. "She'll tell you she's quite happy to be . . . er . . . taking the night air with me."

Sarah could hear the oil boss's staccato breathing. "Is this true, Miss Martindale?" he asked her gratingly.

Jacinto's grip on her wrist tightened, and Sarah's mouth turned dry. Everything she had striven to hide was at stake. If she answered in the affirmative her secret was safe. Her throat ached with indecision. She wanted to say yes, but the feel of Jacinto's lips was scorched on her memory and wrenching herself free she choked, stumbling up the steps past Bryce, "I can't think of anywhere I would less rather be!"

Her breathing still painful, she ran without looking back. She ran up the last of the steps and along the path through the grounds. The house lighting was subdued now. She found the nearest door and the curving staircase and with rasping breath at last gained her room.

She fell on the bed in the darkness and lay for several seconds until her panting subsided. Then she rose slowly to face the windows and the night. It would all be over now. Jacinto would have had his say. She had no illusions as to the kind of man he was. Knowing that he had been crossed, he would enjoy telling his tale.

Sarah's eyes were damp with tears. Bryce was there with him now on the cliff steps listening to all he had to say. As she dragged herself around, stripping off her ripped dress and preparing for bed, she knew with a searing pain in her heart that all was lost.

CHAPTER TEN

WHEN the long sleepless hours were at an end Sarah rose and showered and dressed as usual the next morning. White-faced but fully prepared for her dismissal, she closed the door of her room and went downstairs. She went to collect her breakfast tray from the kitchen, smiling away the glances of concern directed her way and blaming the noisy evening of the night before for her pallor.

She ate alone in the sun-filled dining room listening to the sparrows squabbling outside the window. She had no desire for food. It was simply a matter of filling the time until Bryce Taylor's arrival. When the fading leaves of the fruit trees shone like copper in the sun she looked at her watch. He should be in his office now.

Despite her composure she felt her strength draining away from her as she went out of the room and up the stairs. She could hear the cheerful activity in the other offices. She tapped on the door of her own, as was her custom before entering. There was no reply. Her heart knocked in her throat. Did he know who it was and in his disgust prefer not to answer?

With trembling hand she turned the knob and went in. The room was empty. So she was still too early. Her nerves stretched, Sarah paced. She would have liked to get the business over with, and it was already well after nine-thirty.

It was then she saw the memorandum on her desk. She recognised Bryce's scrawl. He told her he expected to be busily engaged with the Ribieros and couldn't say when he would be able to get into the office. He had made a list of the tasks to be completed in his absence.

Pulse pounding, Sarah read and re-read the note. Had he written it last night before the reception? Or had he been in this morning? She tried to recollect if she had heard him, but in the dining room it wasn't possible to tell what cars were coming and going at the front. In an anguish of uncertainty she wondered what she ought to do.

After wrestling with the problem she decided that there was only one course open to her, and that was to wait for Bryce's arrival.

She went to her desk. There was plenty to keep her occupied. And what was the point in sitting around? In a highly strung fashion she worked through the morning accompanied by all the normal sounds of the household, the Valadins' clatter in the kitchen and the technicians tramping up and down the stairs and driving away. In the afternoon a sleepy air descended, but Sarah stuck to her typing doggedly. Never let it be said that she hadn't given of her best at the end.

It was after seven when she had cleared up the last of the oil company business. Exhausted, she had a meal, then went straight to her room. With the minimum of effort she prepared for bed. Having had no sleep the night before she was ready to fall down anywhere. The moment her head touched the pillow she dropped off into a drugged slumber.

Morning came all too soon. The nagging question that woke Sarah was, *would Bryce be in his office today*? A clammy feeling of fear gripped her as she lay with the thought. It came to her like a blow that she couldn't face him this morning. Yesterday, numbed with shock and weariness, she had hardly cared about accepting the inevitable. But that was a whole day away. Last night she had slept and this morning her senses were keenly tuned to what she would have to face.

No, she couldn't go straight to his office. She needed time to get used to the idea.

She washed and dressed in laggardly fashion, finding all kinds of excuses to keep her from going downstairs. When there was no more hanging back she went down and drank a cup of coffee in the dining room. She wanted to get away from the house, but there was no going by the road at the front. There would be too many cars about. The cliffs were the only answer, and she needed the air.

She made her way out, taking the paths with a hollow feeling inside her. She knew it was useless to fool herself with excuses. The fresh breeze was invigorating, but it only brought the fact home to her more that she was running away because she couldn't face the oil boss.

Her eyes bright with unshed tears, she stopped at the top of the steps and tried to regain control of herself in the face of the wind. Wisps of hair blew about round her temples, but she was past caring about her appearance.

The sea was a tumultuous stretch of white-capped waves stirring from its summer sleep, but still benignly forgetful of winter. Deep and blue and secretive, it rolled in from the farthest horizons. Lowering her dull gaze for the first time, Sarah saw a strange new sight out from the beach below.

There were still several little craft bobbing there, most of them belonging to the technicians. Now they looked like mere matchboxes, for out to sea, riding the swell like some huge majestic bird, was a sleek white yacht. Half-heartedly Sarah let her gaze wander over the luxurious structure. She was eyeing the tiered decks and the assortment of masts when a voice said at her elbow, "*Pyramid Lady*. One of the oil company's yachts."

Sarah spun round to find Bryce Taylor standing beside her. He was looking out to sea. Without altering his gaze he continued leisurely, "I put a request in for the *Snow Goose*, a more versatile ship with slightly less tonnage, but they tell me she's doing service at our oil base in the Mexican Gulf."

Sarah stared at him, at that face she had come to know so well; those green eyes which had a way of glowing darkly when he was pleased, the suggestion of grey at his temples and the deep lines etched around his mouth.

Her voice was locked in her throat. He didn't seem to

notice. He said easily, bringing his eyes round to hers at last, "I hope you've got your sea legs. Tomorrow we'll be sailing to Estoril. I'm throwing in everything we've got to crack the last big nut—the Serveras. You'd better pack your most impressive outfits."

Sarah's mind was in a whirl at his words. They didn't make sense. He was acting as though nothing had changed, as though she was still working as his personal assistant. Wildly in her thoughts she tried to unravel the mess.

Where was Jacinto? What had happened between the two of them that night on the steps? How much did the oil boss know? Frantically Sarah tried to find the answer to these questions. And hard on the heels of this cruel dilemma, another thought came to shock her. He had talked about the Serveras as *the last big nut to crack*. Did that mean that the Ribieros, like everyone else, had succumbed to the idea of an oil refinery in Laso? If so she had to get to Senhor Carvalho and beg him to help. Only she and his family knew that the harbour could never belong to Pyramid Oil.

Agonisingly her thoughts swung back to Bryce. How much did he know about her meetings with the Carvalhos? Had Jacinto told him everything? If only she knew! In a torment of uncertainty she tried to read his features. They were inscrutable as he leisurely lit his pipe.

Because she didn't know, she could do nothing but try to behave normally.

"The Serveras?" she said, conscious of her own high-pitched, strained tones. "Didn't someone say they lived in Estoril?"

"That's right," the oil boss nodded. "They're at their villa just outside Laso at the moment. They've agreed to make up a party aboard the *Pyramid Lady*. I think Joaquin Serveras plans to play the host when we get to Estoril." He puffed his pipe. "The round trip should take about five days."

Sarah's mind was racing. This afternoon she was due to

visit the *quinta* for her weekly meeting with Senhor Carvalho. Now, more than ever, she had to make the trip.

Trying to sound casual, she said, above the breeze playing over the cliffs, "I've brought all the work up to date in the office. Would it be all right if I slipped into town this afternoon to pick up a few things for the trip?"

"Of course," he replied. "I'll drive you down myself."

Sarah struggled not to show her alarm at his words. "Oh, please don't trouble!" she stammered. Was he watching her? "I'm sure one of the technicians will give me a lift."

"It's no bother." Bryce tapped his pipe. "I have to go into town this afternoon, anyway." He took her arm and turned back along the path towards the house. Sarah walked beside him, a dreadful apprehension tugging at her insides.

When they reached the grounds and the loggia he said to her afternoon in town. But when she walked furtively out morrow."

Thankfully Sarah hurried away to her room. She spent the rest of the morning sorting out her clothes for the trip. At lunch time, not daring to go into the dining room in case Bryce was there, she begged a tray from the kitchen and took it back up to her room.

She was hoping that Bryce would have forgotten about her afternoon in town. But when she walked furtively out of the front entrance later, he was there waiting beside the car. There was nothing she could do but get in as he held the door for her.

The distance to Laso was less than half an hour by road, but that afternoon the journey seemed interminable to Sarah. She breathed an inward sigh of relief as the first of the fishing cottages appeared.

"Where would you like me to drop you off?" Bryce asked, as they drove up towards the harbour road.

"Oh, the bus square will do," Sarah tried to sound offhand. "I can easily get to the shops from there." With bated breath she waited, half expecting him to offer to drive her into the town centre. But he pulled up where she had suggested and said, opening the door for her to get out, "If I can't get back myself, I'll send one of the men to pick you up here about five."

"Thank you." Distrustfully Sarah stood where she was until he had started up again and driven off. She watched his car climb the hill past the beach, turn towards the wharfs and disappear from view.

She glanced worriedly at her watch. She would have her work cut out to get back by five. Rapidly she moved towards the shopping area. She hoped that Januario wouldn't leave her hanging about too long. But all she could do was drift around and wait for his signal.

Luckily she had only spent ten minutes buying a new face towel in the chemist's when he appeared on the corner as she stepped out. Sharply she swept her glance around the area. There was nothing to be seen but the impersonal bustle of the townspeople.

She caught Januario's eye and followed him down a side alley. She gave no indication that she knew of his secret talk with Jacinto. As he opened the car door for her she thought he lowered his gaze a little sheepishly. Before she stepped into her seat she glanced furtively to right and left along the alley. It was completely empty. She had no intention of relaxing her vigil, however. She kept a close watch on the route through town. As they drove out to the Amorida valley her gaze was glued to the rear window. Nothing happened. The road was deserted. After giving it some thought she decided to say nothing about the Jacinto episode to Senhor Carvalho. It would only add to his troubles.

The vineyards were alive with September activity. It was grape-picking time and the harvesters climbed the terraces with the huge baskets strapped from their heads. Women wore hats and head-cloths against the sun, and the grapes were picked to the rhythm of flutes and drums. Up near the house musicians accompanied the unloading of the overflowing baskets. The simply dressed harvesters danced a kind of reel. Watching on the drive in through the gates, the merriment to Sarah seemed a far cry from her own heavy spirits.

She went straight through to Senhor Carvalho in his study. He received the news of the Ribieros' move to support Pyramid Oil with a frown of deep concern. For long enough Sarah watched him ponder over the map on the desk.

He said finally, "It would seem that everything now hangs in the balance, for us, and for Pyramid Oil. It's up to the Serveras to decide the issue. Money is of no interest to them—they are already millionaires several times over. If they refuse to sell, their land holdings are big enough to stop Taylor."

"But just supposing they don't?" Sarah watched him worriedly.

"Then unfortunately," Senhor Carvalho shrugged, "I and my family will have to confront him with the harbour deeds."

"Is that fair?" Sarah retorted hotly. "After all the months of work he has put in?"

"That was a risk we had to take," Senhor Carvalho said evenly. "No one suspected he would come so near to achieving his aims."

"But there must be some alternative?" Sarah suggested desperately.

"I'm afraid not, Miss Martindale." Though Senhor Carvalho sighed at the unpleasant prospect, the familiar thread of steel was in his voice as he continued. "The harbour is vital to the Carvalho wine industry. Nothing would induce us to part with it."

As though he sensed some of Sarah's unhappiness he smiled and pointed out encouragingly, "All is still not lost. The Serveras are a powerful family. They may appear to be caught in the net of international hospitality, but they are staunchly for the Portuguese. If they say no to the oil refinery there will be nothing the oil boss or Pyramid Oil can do about it."

Sarah nodded wanly. She found scant comfort in Senhor Carvalho's words. Either way Bryce faced defeat. And it would be all of her doing.

She got through the rest of the business as speedily as possible, then set off back to Laso.

Januario dropped her off in a side street in the town. Moving furtively until the car had disappeared, she headed for the shops. She bought wildly, anything that she might find a use for later. She was glad she had loaded herself up, for it was Bryce himself who arrived in the bus square at five o'clock to pick her up.

He eyed her packages and said with a lazy gleam, "Looks like you've had a busy afternoon."

Sarah nodded, but she couldn't smile for the tumultuous thudding of her heart. Was there a double-edged meaning to his comment? Did he have some idea of how she had really spent the afternoon? She looked at his face as he helped her into the car. If only she knew!

They drove back to O Saudade in silence. Sarah was too prostrate with strain to try and make conversation. Bryce swung the wheel and puffed at his pipe, letting the blue smoke drift leisurely out of the window. There was no telling what he was thinking.

CHAPTER ELEVEN

THEY took Eduardo with them on the *Pyramid Lady*. Like all good manservants he accepted the sudden change of environment with the dignity of his station, moving about the decks with smooth efficiency and an impassive countenance. Sarah wished she could have borrowed some of his implacable calm.

She had taken the boarding launch out with the oil boss, praying fervently that something would go wrong so that they would have to cancel the trip. As though to make a mockery of her hopes the sun had shone brilliantly in the blue autumn sky. The sea was choppy but flat, and there were none of the huge rolling breakers that she would like to have seen, making the trip impossible.

The cream of Laso society was on board. The Serveras, those very special people whom the oil company was nursing along in its last feverish push for the oil refinery, had been given the master suite on the top deck. The rest of the guests were housed on the B and C decks below. Sarah's cabin was next to Bryce Taylor's in the promenade area. Richly panelled, and tastefully lit, it was really like a luxurious bedroom with adjoining bathroom facilities of a standard one might find in only the most expensive hotels.

The Valadins were on board. They were busy in the galley below the bar lounge preparing dinner for the guests. Sarah felt better knowing they were there. Despite their culinary fame they were a homely pair and it was a comfort to know that she would have somewhere to retreat should she desire to escape for a moment from the hazards of the oil business.

The ship was manned by an English crew. She had watched the deck hands in white drill jeans and tee-shirts draw up the launch and secure it at the stern before they saild. The skipper on the bridge was a balding man with ruddy sea-weathered features and the crinkly kind of nautical blue eyes which sailors seemed to have.

Sarah had been over most of the ship. Mainly to avoid Bryce she had wandered around the promenade decks and under the awnings on the sun deck where a swimming pool shimmered under the blue sky. In the garden lounge she had fingered the exotic potted plants crowded against the walls and between the armchairs. And from there she had strolled through the bar lounge to the dining room and the galley.

They were sailing south parallel with the coast. The breezes were playful and Sarah had tied a colourful scarf over her hair. As she stood now watching the land, bathed in the golden light of late afternoon, slip silently by her thoughts centred on the Serveras. What were they like? Similar to the other Laso landowners? The Ribieros, for instance, whom she knew now had sold out to Pyramid Oil. Senhor Carvalho had told her that the Serveras were rich and were not interested in selling their land for money. But he had said that about the others. If only she could be sure he was right this time!

An oil refinery was a blot on the landscape and the head of the Serveras family was known to be proudly protective towards Portugal. That was a point in Sarah's favour. Dared she hope it would be enough to swing the pendulum her way? It only needed the Serveras to say no to Pyramid Oil and her troubles would be over. The Carvalhos would be free to go on shipping their wine from Laso and no one need know about the harbour deeds, least of all Bryce Taylor.

Her heart began to thud painfully when she thought of the man she had worked beside all these months. How could she stand by and watch all his hopes wrecked by the Carvalhos? At least the Serveras would save him that humilation. But would they hold out against his persuasive chat? That was something no one knew.

Worriedly Sarah gazed at the windmills in the distance as the yacht rode south to Estoril. Like everyone else she could only await the outcome of the trip.

As nightfall approached the sea became a little rougher. In her cabin Sarah felt the gentle rise and fall of the ship. She hoped she was going to go down with a bout of sea-sickness, and so miss dinner. Much to her disappointment, though the swell continued into the evening, she remained perfectly healthy.

She had no choice but to bathe and dress in preparation for meeting the guests on board. The oil boss had told her to bring her most impressive outfits. She chose a black chiffon gown dotted with peach-coloured roses. It had long see-through sleeves and a broad silk black sash, and a huge peach rose decorated the base of the rather low-cut bosom.

She daren't do anything but look her best. She had to appear to be doing all she could for Bryce. She used a little make-up and a liberal touch of perfume, and with her hair smoothed back in a diamante clip she picked up a black evening bag and went out.

The sea was a glistening black swell under the stars as she walked along the deck towards the bar lounge. In the gaily lit interior the guests were already enjoying the first drink of the evening. Sarah saw Bryce clad in evening attire; dark suit, white dress shirt and black bow tie. He came to meet her as she joined the throng, his gaze locking with hers in an odd way before he slid an arm round her waist.

He introduced her to the Serveras and walked with her amongst the other Laso guests, many of whom she was already well acquainted with. A little later they went in to dinner.

The dining area was tastefully lit with separate circular tables dotting the carpeted spaces. Sarah noted that each table seated around eight guests. As she might have expected the Serveras were placed at the same table as herself and Bryce. Joaquin Serveras was a gross man with a huge beak of a nose, but his humorous eyes were bright with some kind of tender inner emotion, and they had a way of lighting up when he talked which made one forget his ugly face.

Sarah studied the couple closely during the meal. Many businessmen were influenced by their wives' views, but not Joaquin Serveras. He was not blind to his own power, and Rita Serveras, the type who enjoyed the small talk that women indulge in, was obviously content to let him make up his own mind on important matters.

The oil boss knew better than to try and impress the pair with the superlative qualities of *Pyramid Lady*, a ship they could have bought with their weekly pocket money had they so desired. Instead he used his rugged charm and knowledge of Portugal to pave the way to greater things.

Sarah watched Joaquin Serveras. He spoke with fire when discussing the various facets of his own country, and though the subject of the oil refinery wasn't broached she felt sure his own inclinations, being a lover of beauty and tranquility, were to say no to the project.

If only she could sway him completely in some way, secretly, by her looks or by her smile. Perhaps if she waited for the right moment . . . She took a sip from her wine glass and carefully placed it down. But as she watched him, how did she know Bryce wasn't watching her? No. She lowered her gaze to her plate. That was too dangerous a game, one she dared not risk playing.

As the meal progressed she made an effort to be pleasant over her inner quandaries. She didn't go out of her way to engage Senhor Serveras' attention but he seemed taken with her in some way, and elderly though he was, he flaunted a kind of gallantry as he chatted to her across the table.

He was mainly concerned with expounding the virtues of

Portugal. “And what have you seen of our country so far, Miss Martindale?” he asked her as Eduardo came to take the dessert dishes away.

“Not a lot,” Sarah smiled. “I’ve been rather busy, I’m afraid.”

“We must alter that,” he boomed, puffing on his tremendous cigar. “No one comes to Portugal without seeing Sintra. ‘Glorious Eden’, your Byron called it, and that’s what it is. You see if you don’t agree. I’ll take you there myself,” he told her with enthusiastic fervour.

Just say ‘No’ to the oil refinery, Sarah tried to tell him with her eyes. That will be enough for me. But, lost to her pleas, he rambled on about the various beauty spots up and down the country and she could only hope that he was dropping a large hint to the oil boss as to his real views on the matter.

After dinner the guests retired to the sun-deck lounge. Screened off now to shut out the night breezes, a smooth dance floor had been laid over the pool and in keeping with the starlit sea gleaming through the transparent screens, soft music drifted out over the hidden speakers.

Sarah danced with Bryce. What else could she do? The guests were made up of couples, so it was only natural that they should pair up. He wasn’t a dancing man, nor had she had much practice, but they moved around slowly to the music and no one would have suspected that they had no idea of the steps.

Bryce held her close to him. Sometimes she felt his cheek brushing her hair. She longed to lean against him, but the awful weight of her troubles made her dance most of the time with her heart in her throat.

It was late when the party broke up. Happy with the way the evening had turned out, the guests drifted away to their respective cabins. Sarah’s cabin was next to that of the oil boss, so what more natural than that they should go that way together?

Before they left the promenade deck they stopped for

a moment in the darkness to watch the glistening swell of the waves beyond the ship. Bryce drew Sarah close against him. She felt his lips trailing along her throat. She would have given all she possessed to turn her mouth to his, but, all too conscious of the disaster looming on the horizon for him, she pulled away from him and fled to her cabin.

Breakfast was a leisurely affair with the guests drifting in and out of the dining room as they felt like it. Sarah drank a cup of coffee at the rail side, then, because she had no special duties until later when there was to be a clay-pigeon shoot, she escaped for a while to the galley below the bar lounge.

The Valadins were enjoying the trip tremendously. They seemed to work even better aboard ship and already their exotic food displays for the day's meals were taking shape. Sarah found Lucia's cheery chat soothing to her troubled mind. She helped with the salad dressing and the whipped cream decoration, listening to the woman's garrulous, accented English with a worn smile. Attractive in a mature way with her flashing eyes and black, tightly drawn back hair, Lucia was agog this morning with some excitement that seemed to be percolating around the ship.

She said to Sarah with a conspiratorial air as they were arranging glazed fruits in patterns on a tray, "How did Senhor Serveras look at dinner last night?"

"Fine." Sarah eyed her with a puzzled gaze.

"Did he eat the shellfish-stuffed crepes, and the souffle Rothschild?" Lucia queried anxiously.

"As far as I know he enjoyed everything put before him. Why?" Sarah licked the sugar off her fingers.

"Well, because it's very important to treat him nice." Lucia raised her eyebrows in surprise at Sarah's apparent ignorance. And in a whispered aside, "If he says yes to the oil refinery there's a fat bonus in it for all of us. Why do you think the crew are on their best behaviour?"

Sarah pondered on her words. She had noticed the

impeccable performance of the ship's crew whenever there were tasks to be undertaken. Lucia giggled, adding the last touch to the tray. "We're all working with our hearts in our mouths!"

No more than she was, Sarah told herself miserably. Lucia wiped her fingers and tossed the cloth on to the table. The bonus payment was already in her pocket as she lapsed dreamily, "I've seen an adorable little dress in Mateus' in Laso . . ."

"What for you want another dress?" Her husband asserted himself across the flour-caked table. "Already we have no room for all your clothes."

"So!" Her hands on her hips, Lucia flared at him in her hot-blooded way, then smiled equably. "We will find more room!"

Sarah left them to their affectionate bickering. The pigeon shoot was about to commence and she had to be there to give the oil boss moral support. As she went up the steps Lucia called after her, "Whatever you do, don't upset Senhor Serveras!"

"I'll try not to." Sarah made an effort to sound light-hearted, but up on deck her spirits dropped to their lowest ebb. It seemed that everybody was pulling for Pyramid Oil. Everybody except her.

Down on the well deck the wives were gathering excitedly to watch the prowess of their respective husbands with sporting rifles. Tables and chairs had been arranged in the lee of the wind, and the sprucely turned-out deck hands hovered expectantly over the firing contraption and loaded rifles.

Everyone was waiting for Senhor Serveras. He came at last, walking and talking earnestly with Bryce Taylor. Despite his great girth and huge frame he managed to give a picture of elegance in his pale striped beach slacks and fawn cashmere windcheater. He laughed and joked, thoroughly enjoying the blunders that some of the men made when the shooting began.

The firing contraption made a fearful noise and Sarah kept well back in her corner behind Bryce. Each man had a round of six. He had to be very fast to take aim, fire and secure a direct hit all in the split-second in which the clay pigeon was released. Each shooter's score was carefully chalked up on a board by a deck-hand. The average was between three and five hits.

Senhor Serveras, grunting and hopping around and obviously a keen sportsman, judging by his laughing remarks, couldn't wait to show the rest of them how it was done. Despite his elderly appearance he had amazingly quick reflexes. With almost effortless ease he disintegrated one clay pigeon after another as it was fired into the air. There seemed to be no holding him. Three ... four ... five direct hits he notched up. When his sixth clay pigeon exploded in splinters in the air a roar of applause went up on the ship.

Basking in the glory of his success, Senhor Serveras mopped his brow and chuckled with unabashed self-satisfaction at his skill. He eyed Bryce with a challenging glint as the latter took his place at the rail. Sarah had thought the older man was quick, but she hadn't seen the oil boss in action.

Athletic in sailcloth slacks and blue gaberdine jacket, he took aim and fired as the pigeons were catapulted into the air, with such well-oiled precision one hardly saw the movement of his finger on the trigger. One . . . two . . . three . . . he shattered the flying objects speeding out to sea as though they had been toy kites floating on the breeze. Four . . . five . . . Was there the fraction of a pause before he fired his last shot? Sarah thought there was. He aimed, fired, and missed, and a roar of sympathy rose among the onlookers.

Senhor Serveras was delighted at his lapse. "O ho! Bad luck, Bryce," he chortled, doing a dance of victory. The oil boss grinned ruefully as the older man slapped him on the back, but Sarah wasn't deceived. She knew he could have splintered that last pigeon with perfect ease if he had wanted to.

The men drifted off to the bar and Sarah watched Bryce's departure with a wry glance. She was well aware of his tactics. Like everyone else aboard the *Pyramid Lady* he was taking care not to upset Senhor Serveras.

The yacht sailed into Estoril with its palm-lined promenades and graceful villas, in the mellowing light of late afternoon. Dinner was taken on board, after which the guests crowded into the launch for a night at the Casino. The men were dressed in dinner jackets, the women in gowns befitting the occasion.

Sarah had put on a dress of saffron silk decorated with lace. To ward off the chill night air she had draped a white stole around her shoulders. She was helped into the launch, on its second trip, by Bryce and stood beside him as the craft sped over the waves. Unlike the other guests, chattering and laughing at the thought of the evening to come, she viewed the prospect of several hours ashore with black dismay. Her nerves felt as brittle as glass from the long-drawn-out agony of waiting to hear the worst about the oil refinery. While everyone looked forward to the visit to the gaming rooms and the trip to Sintra the following day, she spent her time wishing the wretched business was over.

Of course she had to be careful not to let her misery show. Later when they approached the Casino with its floodlit gardens, statues and imposing entrance, and Senhor Serveras took her arm, eager to show her as much as possible in the time allowed, she tried to put on a look of bright expectancy.

They went straight to the gaming rooms, softly lit interiors with illuminated green baize tables. Croupiers in royal blue dinner jackets supervised at the tables and above the hum of voices could be heard the steady click-click of the roulette wheels.

Senhor Serveras was obviously a very important patron of the gambling salon, for he was bowed to by the distinguished-looking chief croupier and several stewards rushed forward to do his bidding. In expansive mood, he ordered little baskets of chips to be given to all the guests in his party. Sarah hadn't the faintest idea what to do with hers. She had never been in a gaming room in her life, and money meant nothing to her in her present frame of mind.

But Senhora Serveras knew nothing of her emotional stress. He wanted to show her all there was to the business of gambling, and to humour the man she did as he told her at the various tables around the room. She thought if she lost all her chips quickly she would be allowed to escape, but instead she won all the time. She just couldn't get rid of the darn things! As fast as she piled them on to a number, or a combination of numbers, someone else was piling more her way.

Senhor Serveras was delighted at her good luck, especially as he had a hand in it. He ordered a bigger basket to hold her chips and as he helped her to scoop them in Sarah caught the dry gleam of the oil boss standing beside her.

When he became bored with the roulette wheels Senhor Serveras beckoned his party to follow and they were led to a white roped-off area where a solitary croupier welcomed their arrival. Close beside the big man who was heartily ushering her on, Sarah kept a smile on her face, though inwardly she shrank at the sight of yet another green baize table. Oh dear! Now it was going to be cards.

Paying little attention to the rules as they were explained to her, she joined in pretending to get as big a thrill out of the game as the rest of the party seemed to do. She played, but her mind was racing around on other things. It meant nothing to her that hers was the biggest pile of chips on the table. She squandered them liberally at every opportunity, hardly noticing that the pile in the centre was growing larger by the minute. She was lost too to the fact that the couples were dropping out one by one from the bidding as the game progressed. Perhaps, because of her distracted state, the worry and anxiety mounting within her, she was blind to so much that was going on around the table. She had a number of cards in her hand, and so had Senhor Serveras. It didn't register on her troubled mind that they were now the only two playing, or if it did, it didn't appear to be important.

If she had given more to the game beside her smile she would have felt the tension mounting around the table, sensed the fire of challenge in Senhor Serveras's gaze. He was a man who derived a sense of power from winning at the gaming tables and in beating his opponents. But Sarah didn't know that. She was mainly concerned with getting rid of the last of her chips, and this she did by scooping them on to the pile in the centre of the table.

When this brought a snort of frustration from the older man and made him lay his cards on the table, she was hardly aware that she was supposed to do the same. She did, slowly, and an uproar rose around the table. There were laughing cries of "bluffing!" and "fraud!" as everyone looked at her low score as opposed to the kings and queens across the table.

It was only then that Sarah realised her blunder. Her cheeks burned. As they turned to go she dared not look at Bryce. She knew now that in the reckless squandering of her chips she had done the unforgivable. She had outbid Senhor Serveras.

Most of the guests went back to the *Pyramid Lady*. Sarah and Bryce, along with one or two others, had been invited to spend the night at the Serveras' palatial residence on the sea front. Sarah viewed the ornate structure like a huge birthday cake in design with subdued amazement as they approached by the light of the stars.

She spent the night in a bedroom with a domed ceiling, colourfully decorated with cupids and garlands of flowers, and breakfasted in bed the next morning from a silver tray, itself not lacking in embellishments. As she lay back amongst the pillows and viewed the opulence around her, her heart began to beat a little lighter. With all this, why should Joaquin Serveras be tempted to relinquish his hold on a few dozen acres of land at Laso?

She dressed in the day clothes she had brought with her from the yacht, a rose-pink shirt-blouse and wide-belted skirt, and went down to join the guests who would be arriving from the *Pyramid Lady*.

A fleet of cars had been hired to take the party to Sintra. In a seat beside Bryce in the leading limousine Sarah had a perfect view on the seven-mile drive towards the jagged mountain range.

Sintra nestled at the foot of the pine-clad slopes. One peak, capped by two castles towered directly above the town. The stucco houses, softened by time, gleamed red, blue, pink and orange in the morning sunshine.

The cars arrived in the main square and as the guests alighted Sarah learned that their destination was the National Palace. Joaquin Serveras, his defeat of the night before apparently forgotten, escorted her on the walk. She was flattered that he had arranged the trip for her benefit and over the gnawing worry inside her she tried to appear intensely interested in all he showed her. Had his wife been a jealous woman she might have taken umbrage at the way he openly flirted with Sarah, but being a mature woman she smiled at his antics with affectionate tolerance.

He wanted Sarah to see everything and pointed out to her the luxurious vegetation as they walked. She was vaguely stirred at the beauty of camellias, and ferns, dripping pink bougainvillea, strawberry beds, red geraniums and lizards crawling over the damp tiled walls.

Tickets had to be bought at the Palace, but Senhor Serveras swept his guests forward and no one tried to deter him. He was obviously a very important man in Portugal. Sarah's heart dropped when she saw the size of the twin-spired structure they were expected to tour. She longed to drop back beside the oil boss who was following close behind her, but Senhor Serveras was doing all this for her and she dared not openly upset him.

She tried, as far as she could, to be an eager listener to all he told her about the Palace as he led her through the vast vaulted interior. She saw the Room of the Swans and learned that its window decoration had come from Spanish Morocco. And the Stag Room with its coats-of-arms of the noble families of Portugal, and scenes from the hunt. She saw the graceful Room of the Mermaids and the original tiled stove in the old kitchen.

From many of the salons Senhor Serveras pointed out to her the excellent vistas opening onto the hills surrounding Sintra. To Sarah, the tapestries, paintings, sheltered patios, softly falling water, potted plants and long dark corridors evoked the faded life of another era. She couldn't say she wasn't impressed by all she had seen, but she was glad when the party at last began to make their way back to the cars.

For her benefit they went on another route back. Now more than ever as they walked, the greenness of Sintra made itself felt on Sarah; its dark green trees with vine bound trunks, clear streams bubbling over rocks coated with rich velvet moss; lichen the colour of young olives clinging to every tree. She felt too the fierce pride in Joaquin Serveras as he pointed out to her his favourite things, and suddenly her heart lifted again. Loving all this as he did, she was sure he would never consent to anything as ugly as an oil refinery.

As they arrived at the cars in the square her eyes rested tenderly on Bryce. If only she could be just as sure that everything would turn out right for him!

CHAPTER TWELVE

THE afternoon sun caught the waves and lit their spray in rainbow hues as they fell away from the ship. The dull hum of the engines rose above their swishing sound and the cry of seagulls flying far out from land. Unknown to the guests there was an air of tension aboard the *Pyramid Lady*. Everyone was waiting for Senhor Serveras' decision. Sarah felt it stronger than the others. For her everything depended on it.

The guests were resting in their cabins, but, too overwrought to stay indoors, she had come to stand at the rail as the ship sped north, bound for Laso. The last thing she wanted was company, but hearing a heavy footstep along the deck and turning to see the skipper Harry Stockton making towards her, she knew he was looking for someone to talk to. He was a cheerful man and she had spoken to him once or twice in the company of the oil boss. There was nothing she could do but wait for him to join her.

"Have you enjoyed the trip, Miss Martindale?" he asked her as he approached in his stolid, hearty fashion.

"Very much, thank you, Mr. Stockton," Sarah tried to sound pleasant.

He leaned beside her at the rail and viewing the sea with his crinkly knowledgeable gaze told her, "We should be in Laso this time tomorrow if all goes well."

"What will you do then?" Sarah smiled, knowing he wanted her to pursue the subject.

The skipper pushed his peaked cap to the back of his head so that his thinning hair was flicked in the breeze. "The crew will be entitled to a few hours' shore leave," he grinned, "then we'll head back to home base in Southampton."

"Will it be a rough trip?" Sarah asked mechanically, her mind already gnawing again at her own problems.

"No, I don't think so." The blue eyes scanned the ocean professionally. Then after some thought, "Could be tricky in the bay."

"The bay?" Sarah queried absently, wondering with knotted insides if Senhor Serveras had arrived at a decision yet.

"Biscay," the skipper told her, and proceeded to ramble on. "And Finisterre can be rough. But once we get across to Brest the going gets easier. From there the *Pyramid Lady* will practically sail herself."

"Which means you'll soon be home," Sarah smiled over the nagging worries inside her.

The skipper looked at the sky in a way that sailors do and said with the experience of years, "Sailing by the evening tide tomorrow we should do it in three days at the outside." He was in a talkative mood and went on to tell Sarah more about the sea routes and snags to be avoided. Hardly giving an ear to what he was saying, she was glad when a member of the crew came to tell him he was wanted on the bridge.

Dinner aboard the *Pyramid Lady* was a gay affair for everyone except Sarah. There was no doubt that the ordeal of the past few days was beginning to have a disastrous effect on her nerves, but, dressed in white chiffon, her gleaming hair caught at the nape of her neck in a spangled net, she tried to appear serene at the dinner table.

The meal lingered well into the evening, after which the men took themselves off with their cigars and brandy glasses, and the women amused themselves in groups around the garden lounge. Bryce had gone off with Joaquin Serveras and it was Sarah's job to see that his wife was suitably entertained. At a corner table with one or two other elderly members of the party she sat and chatted pleasantly with Senhora Serveras over coffee. At bedtime Sarah rose to accompany the older woman down the room to where the men were.

Joaquin Serveras was puffing on the last of his cigar, his great bulk spilling over the armchair he relaxed in. Bryce sat a little to the side of him. Sarah followed Rita Serveras to the armchairs opposite them.

Throughout the evening she had barely been able to control the wild thudding of her heart as she had watched the two men deep in conversation. Her one thought had been the oil refinery. It was obvious they had been hammering it out, for as she took her seat now they were still talking on the subject.

Senhora Serveras settled back amiably, content to let the conversation wash over her while she waited for her husband to retire. Sarah, trying to give a similar picture of tranquility, listened with bated breath. She heard Bryce reply forcefully to something the other man had said, "Oh, come now, Joaquin, a scheme like this can give employment to thousands, and possibly attract immigrants back from abroad. What's bad about that for Portugal? It means prosperity for the people of Laso and improved standards all round. It can only create stability."

"But an oil refinery is such an ugly thing," Senhor Serveras said in dogged tones.

"Was," the oil boss fired back. "Nowadays we go in for landscaping on a big scale. With what we have in mind we can mask the site from every angle but the sea."

Senhor Serveras sighed and looked thoughtful. With his gallant gleam roaming over to Sarah he asked good-naturedly, "And what does Miss Martindale think about it?"

Sarah smiled, reclining back in her chair. "Well, Fawley in England, which is not far from where I live, has a huge oil refinery. I hardly ever notice it. There's only the flame-stacks to be seen, and then only at night." She paused for breath. Why she was talking like this she didn't know, but she couldn't stop herself. "Lymington," she went on, "the pretty little harbour town similar to Laso, across the river, didn't suffer at all. If anything it has improved tremendously by the money the oil industry has brought into the area."

Senhor Serveras puffed leisurely on the stub of his cigar then stubbed it out in the ash tray. The lounge was empty and after one or two more exchanges the men got to their feet.

Sarah escorted Senhora Serveras to the door and out to the staircase of their master suite. She left the two men talking by the rail and escaped to her cabin, a wry smile on her face. No one could say she wasn't the perfect personal assistant!

They arrived in Laso mid-afternoon the following day. The sun shone warmly from a clear sky as the *Pyramid Lady* dropped anchor in the stretch of water facing O Saudade.

After a morning spent taking the sea air and a lunch of the Valadins' very special *sole meunière* the guests piled into the launch for the relay trips to shore.

The Serveras were the first to leave. The oil boss and several spruced-up members of the crew escorted them in style on the run. Checking that nothing had been left behind and assisting each couple in the party with their bits and pieces, Sarah was one of the last to leave the ship. She sailed as the afternoon began to fade, with the rest of the crew who had been invited to spend a few hours at O Saudade.

As soon as they reached the house she went straight to her room. The last of the guests had long since departed and for once she could be alone. Worn out after the culmination of the days of anxiety, she unpacked simply because she couldn't bear to sit around. When that was finished she tackled other jobs even though her body cried out for rest. She dared not give herself time to think or the brittle film of composure which held her together might shatter completely. Only when the light began to fade did she leave her room on the pretext of going in search of some refreshment.

The technicians were larking about in the doorways of the oil offices before leaving for the day. Sarah was struck by their jaunty mood. As she went downstairs she came upon a group of crew members from the yacht engaged in a tustle in the hall. Others were romping out on the lawns in the last of the light. Ignoring everyone's high spirits, Sarah made her way through the house, trying not to hear the little warning bell of alarm which sounded inside her.

In the kitchen the Valadins were rushing around preparing mountains of food. Sarah's insides tightened up as she watched Lucia, red-faced and shining-eyed, putting the finishing touches to a tremendous gateau. She poured herself a cup of coffee and tried to sound casual. "Someone's in for a treat."

"It's for the crew of the *Pyramid Lady,*" Lucia giggled. "Senhor Bryce has given orders to serve them a banquet in the dining room to celebrate."

"Celebrate?" Sarah echoed faintly.

"Haven't you heard?" Lucia scooped up a fingerful of cream and licked on it delightedly. "Senhor Serveras has sold his land to Pyramid Oil!"

Sarah felt the life drain out of her. She clutched at the table to save herself from crumpling. Making an effort to lower her coffee cup carefully amidst the bustle, she tried to sound lighthearted. "In that case I'd better let you get on with your work."

Blindly she made her way through the darkening rooms of the house. The worst had happened! Pyramid Oil had won. And she had been the last one to learn of their victory. She stumbled on, not knowing which way to turn, then a sight through a ground floor window made her freeze in her tracks.

A black car had pulled up on the drive outside. It was a car that Sarah knew well. She watched Senhor Carvalho step out, briefcase in hand. He was accompanied by his sons. Grim-faced, they went inside.

Sarah clutched at the curtains for support. Of course! They wouldn't need her to tell them the news. The whole of Laso would be rocked with it by now. Standing by for the return of the *Pyramid Lady*, they would have driven straight here from the *quinta*.

She shrank back as she heard their footsteps on the stairs. They had come to see the oil boss. Having been in conference with his technicians he would still be in his office.

With her heart thudding in her throat she waited until she heard the office door close upstairs behind them. On trembling legs she made her way up to her room. Once inside she moved around in a wild panic, not knowing what to do first. She had to get away—anywhere away from Bryce. She would never be able to face him again.

Trying to think clearly, she stuffed her tweed suits into an embroidered bag, and the paltry few possessions she had brought out with her to Portugal. Jerking the cord tight, she put the light out and opened the door. All was in darkness. Across from the stairs a light shone under the office door. She could hear voices; the oil boss's and Senhor Carvalho's. Weak with fear, she tiptoed past, expecting the door to be flung open on her. Once downstairs she fled outside and along the path to the gates.

Away from the house the road was dark. The cars relied on their headlights until they approached the town. As she stumbled along Sarah thought her best plan would be to make for Porto. But she had to get to Laso first. She toyed with the idea of begging a lift and immediately discarded it. All the cars on this road would be oil company cars. No, she would have to get there somehow alone.

A sound up ahead made her tense. At the faint gleam of headlights she panicked and ran into the trees at the side of the road. The way was steep, but the car was sliding by and she was terrified of being seen. She fled on a downward path until all was in darkness again.

When her eyes became accustomed to the gloom she

could make out the pale strip of beach below, and out to sea the ghostly shape of the *Pyramid Lady* riding the waves. Nothing stirred on the road now, but Sarah didn't turn back in that direction. She kept going on the rough downhill route. A plan was forming in her mind.

Down on the beach, the waves tumbled noisily over the sand. A white shape was beached below the steps of the house in the distance. Her feet sank in the soft sand as Sarah struggled in the darkness towards it.

She approached the launch warily, then seeing that it was unattended she hurried towards it. There was a plank in position. She staggered along it and almost fell into the boat. In the gloom she was terrified that she was going to meet up with some figure inside, but the cabin was empty. The boat was waiting for the crew who would be dining now at O Saudade.

Shattered, Sarah sat down on a seat to wait. With only the stars above her she had plenty of time to ponder on what would be going on in the oil offices. Her throat ached when she thought of Bryce and the anger and frustration he must be feeling now.

It was all a hopeless mess. Damp-eyed, she swallowed painfully, looking back, and wondering what she could have done to avoid it. There were lots of things, of course. She shouldn't have taken the job in the first place. But if she hadn't . . . The tears that threatened made her eyes shine brilliantly when she thought of all these months working close beside Bryce Taylor. How could she have lived without them? And how was she going to? . . . She closed her eyes over the unbearable thought of never seeing him again and tried not to think of the bleak days ahead.

Lost in a world of despair, she paid no attention to the time. It was the sound of voices and shouts of laughter coming down the cliffside that made her start up in a fresh bout of panic. That would be the crew returning to the ship.

Wildly she searched around for somewhere to hide. The storm locker in the cabin was cluttered with oilskins. There was room enough amongst them. With her bag she climbed inside and pulled the door to behind her. Her thudding heart almost stifled her as she listened to the heavy footsteps approaching over the sand.

Amidst the jollity the boat had to be launched. Suffocating in the locker, she heard the bawdy shouts of merriment as the men heaved to get it afloat. Amongst the oilskins she felt herself rocking, then there was a thudding and a scuffling as the men clambered aboard. The floorboards beneath her feet vibrated as the engine started. There was a jerk forward and she heard the waves slapping around them as the launch sped out to sea.

After only minutes the engines were slackening again. She guessed they were coming alongside the *Pyramid Lady*. There was much shouting and manoeuvring, after which she heard the men's footsteps clumping around again and then gradually receding as they climbed aboard the yacht.

She held her breath as the launch bobbed and rocked on the water with only her on board. She was struck with the horrible feeling that they might leave her there, marooned. Hysteria rose within her and she was on the point of rushing out when there was the clumping sound of footsteps again and someone jumped down into the boat. She heard the clanging sound of grappling hooks being fixed, then the shout from beside her in the launch was answered by someone above.

The whining note of an engine struck up. There was the clang of chains. Slowly Sarah felt herself and the launch rising out of the water as it was hauled aboard the yacht. Suspended, she waited, and eventually there came the familiar noise of the locking of the ratchets as the launch was secured aboard the yacht. From her stifling hiding place she heard the crew member jump down on to the deck and join others who were moving about the ship.

Amidst the commotion of winding up the anchor and

preparing to sail Sarah opened the door of the locker for air. But that was all. Not until much later when the engines of *Pyramid Lady* were throbbing rhythmically did she climb out stiffly into the cabin of the launch.

Through the glass windows she caught the eerie view of the dimly lit coastline away in the distance, rising and falling with the motion of the ship. Outside the force of the breeze hit her. The decks below her were in darkness apart from odd pools of light here and there. The only sounds to be heard were the lonely swish of the waves against the side, and the steady hum of the engines.

Sarah climbed down from the launch with difficulty, and stood swaying on the deck for several minutes from the effort. When she had gathered enough strength she made her way calmly towards the garden lounge. She was still wearing the rose-pink shirt-blouse and wide-belted skirt she had donned that morning to combat the sea breezes. The outfit was doubly useful now in warding off the chill night air.

She had almost made the door of the lounge when a crew member came whistling nonchalantly down a flight of steps at the side, a young man with a shock of tumbling blonde hair. He stopped and stared at her as though she were an apparition, and then backed away. Sarah tried to give him a smile of reassurance, but his startled gaze fixed on her he turned and stumbling into things he hurried away.

Wearily she made her way into the lounge. She was standing watching the progress of the ship through the windows when hearing a scrabble of footsteps behind she turned to find the skipper staggering to a halt in the doorway.

Like the crew member he eyed her with a stunned look, but being a mature man he quickly covered up his surprise and said with a show of ease, "Why, Miss Martindale! This is an unexpected pleasure."

Sarah gave him a pleading look. "I have to get to

England," she said with a rush. And with an attempt at a smile, "I thought you wouldn't mind if I thumbed a lift."

The skipper looked uncomfortable. "It's a little irregular . . ."

"I know," Sarah said quickly, "but I won't be any trouble." She begged with her eyes. The skipper pursed his lips. He backed off from her as the crew member had done. As he made for the door Sarah sank down and said in grateful tones, "I'd appreciate it if you said nothing of this to the oil company."

"Please feel free to make use of the facilities aboard." The skipper nodded and turning, went out.

In her armchair Sarah felt the weariness wash over her. A few minutes later a steward came to make her coffee at the bar. He placed the tray on the table beside her and went out.

Sarah sipped slowly and when her coffee was finished she remained slumped in the chair, too numb with unhappiness to stir. It was after midnight when she finally looked at her watch. She supposed she ought to go and find herself a cabin for the night. On legs that felt like rubber she made her way out.

In the darkness outside she went to stand at the rail and listened to the thud and boom of the waves against the ship's side. She was on her way to England. But was that what she wanted?

Eyes bright with tears she looked at the twinkling lights of the coastline in the distance. Somewhere back there the lights of O Saudade might still be shining up on the cliff. On a wave of longing she strained her gaze backwards in the darkness, probing, searching through the dazzle of tears.

There was one very bright light back there. As Sarah gazed at it she had a curious feeling it was moving. Whether it was her wet eyes that were distorting the image she couldn't have said, but it seemed to be growing larger all the time.

Her gaze still searching for O Saudade, the radiance from the moving light began to cloud her vision. It appeared to be a small craft of some kind on the water. It was moving very fast, heading this way.

Sarah felt what little strength she had drain away from her. She watched the light grow bigger and bigger. It began to flash on and off as it approached. Someone was sending signals of some kind. She clutched the rail, and as she did so the engines of *Pyramid Lady*, which had been thudding along rhythmically, suddenly shuddered, slowed down and gradually grinded to a halt.

In the awful silence that descended Sarah stood white-faced and tense. Its flashing lights full on the craft was speeding in. It gained easily on the now stationary yacht, and with a dreadful roar of its engines it slewed in, in a wide arc, and thundered alongside on a plume of foam. It was a high-powered speedboat similar to the ones Sarah had seen moored out from the beach in Laso.

She didn't need to look to see who was climbing out down there on to the steps of the *Pyramid Lady*. As the sound of footsteps came up to her she backed away along the deck, looking around wildly for an escape. But there was no shutting out that familiar tread. It was approaching rapidly.

With panic in her throat Sarah began to run, and as she did so the decks were suddenly flooded with light, as the yacht blazed with illumination. White and trembling, she rushed on and was brought to a halt at the prow of the ship. There was nowhere left to run to.

Like a trapped animal she turned at the rail and watched as Bryce Taylor came into view. Now there was only the water below her, black and swirling . . . She turned back to gaze down at it in a hypnotised fashion and that voice that she knew so well ripped out across the deck. "Sarah! Stay where you are!"

As he approached her the tortured look on his face cleared and in an odd cracked tone that was somehow laced with gentleness he said, "Come here, you fool woman. I've had every man in the company out looking for you!"

He had? Clutching the rail, Sarah blinked at him in wonder. Something in his gaze drew her towards him. He put out his arms and gathered her to him. Then in full view of the skipper on the bridge and all the crew, he kissed her long and tenderly.

When Sarah opened her eyes they reflected the glow of the stars. Her wonder increased as she looked at the face of the oil boss. He didn't hate her after all. Or if he did, he had a peculiar way of showing it.

Feeling a bubbling happiness, she laughed, puzzled. "But . . . I don't understand. Haven't you seen Senhor Carvalho? Didn't he show you the harbour deeds?"

"You mean these?" With a grin the oil boss reached into his breast pocket and pulled out an envelope.

Sarah stared at the familiar documents and gasped, "You have them!" And then with concern, "What are the Carvalhos going to do?"

"Go on shipping their wine as usual," he smiled, thrusting the deeds back into his pocket. He drew Sarah towards him again, then cocking a humorous glint up at the rows of eyes trained on them he guided her away to a secluded corner.

Quite uncomprehending and burning with her own guilt, Sarah asked him as they stood sheltered from the wind, "Did you know that I was working for the Carvalhos?"

"Not exactly." Bryce gave her his lopsided smile. "I suspected something was going on when you came to me for a job. Especially as I had seen you at the hotel that first morning."

"You saw me!" Sarah echoed, thunderstruck.

Bryce nodded. "You were asking for your bill at the desk. I passed you on the way out to my car."

"And I never knew," Sarah mused aloud.

"Just to be on the safe side," Bryce turned his arms

round her waist, "I instructed the oil company to look for an alternative harbour. They found one on the wild stretch of coast just north of Laso."

"But the Carvalhos said another harbour in the district was out of the question," Sarah replied in surprise.

The oil boss grinned. "They've no idea of the vast amounts of money and scientific equipment available to the oil company for these ventures. The new harbour's too small for the oil refinery, but it's nearer to the Carvalhos' vineyard by road. As it means a considerable cut in their fuel bills they're more than happy with it."

Sarah glowed at the news. "I can't believe it!" she laughed. "It's like some wild and wonderful dream! Pyramid Oil gets its oil refinery, and the Carvalhos get a brand new harbour."

"And even I get what I want," Bryce said drily, and drew Sarah close to him. His eyes were dark with the love she had seen hovering there these past few weeks. As his lips found hers she had no complaints.

A long time later he said, close against her, "The times I've wanted to do that! But you were always so remote and unapproachable."

"I thought the same about you." Sarah clung to him.

"And self-sufficient too," he went on sternly, as though he was still with his own thoughts. "On our week-end in Lisbon I wanted to show you the sights, but you went off on your own and stayed out the whole day on Sunday. I happen to know, because I knocked on your door several times."

"You did!" Sarah's eyes glowed as she watched him. Then they narrowed as she asked smoothly, "And what about Miss Maggie la Fay? You were quite taken with her. Or so it seemed."

He sloped a smile. "Maggie's just an old friend. I drove her to her night club, and met some colleagues there who were down for the oil conference. I went back to their hotel and we talked shop until the early hours."

He brushed his lips against Sarah's and drawled, "What did you get up to that Sunday?"

"I got lost," Sarah said drily, "wandering through some narrow alleys down by the river."

"The Alfalma district?" Bryce searched her face and drew her close. "That's not a good place for a woman." He added with a gleam, "If I'd known I'd have come and rescued you."

Sarah smiled. "That kind of thing only happens in books."

"Oh, I don't know," Bryce said with a lazy glint. "I came and sorted Jacinto out, didn't I?"

"Jacinto!" Sarah shuddered at the name. "Whatever happened to him?"

"He struck me as being a shady character," Bryce said vibrantly. "When we went to the wine cellars I noticed that the metal tags on the barrels had been tampered with. I made a few enquiries and discovered that he was ordering his barrels from various coopers, changing the tags to the company mark and putting his own price on the invoices to swindle his British partners."

"So that was how he made his extra money," Sarah breathed in shocked tones.

Bryce nodded. "When he came to me with his tale that night on the cliff steps about you working for the Carvalhos, I told him I knew his game. I threatened to report him to his British partners unless he left the district." The oil man smiled grimly. "You won't be seeing Jacinto in these parts again. Rumour has it he's gone to seek his fortunes abroad."

Sarah looked into his green eyes and gleamed. "You knew I was working for the Carvalhos. Why didn't you sack me?"

"I found I couldn't," he gleamed back. "As it turned out it was fortunate. You made a big hit with Joaquin Serveras, and I think that swung the deal. Mind you," his arm gripped her as he glinted, "If he tried that now, I'd tell him to keep his eyes off my wife!"

Sarah rested her head on his shoulder and asked dreamily after a while, "What will happen to O Saudade, now that your work is finished?"

"It's ours if you want it," Bryce replied. He added with a crooked grin, "One of the perks of getting an oil refinery launched!"

"But what about your job?" Sarah asked him.

"The oil refinery will need a manager. I've already accepted the position." His voice was vibrant against her ear.

Sarah's heart swelled with happiness. Close to him, she murmured, "I can't believe we're really going to live at O Saudade."

"We'll get rid of the staff for a start and shut the door to visitors," he said drily, trailing his lips along her throat.

She said as an afterthought, "Isn't it a little big for just the two of us?"

"There won't always be just the two of us," he grinned. "You might be glad of a bit of peace and quiet as the rooms begin to fill up."

Averting her gaze shyly, Sarah changed the subject deftly with, "How did you know I was here, on the yacht?"

"The skipper radioed me that he had a stowaway on board," came the lazy reply.

"I thought he might have to," Sarah sighed, thanking her lucky stars that he did.

Running his lips through her hair, Bryce was lost in his own thoughts again, ". . . there's a certain roof-top restaurant in Lisbon . . . strictly a honeymoon table for two. . ."

Sarah looked at him. "I'll go on one condition," she said sternly.

"What's that?" came his smothered reply.

"That you don't deafen me with the car radio all the way down there this time!"

Bryce raised his gaze to meet her twinkle. He grinned,

"You made me feel uncomfortable. I played the radio loud to retain my bachelor status."

"And what about your bachelor status now?" She quirked an eyebrow at him.

"Hang it!" his grin broadened. "Let's get married—the sooner the better."

Taking her hand, he led her out from their sheltered corner, and slowly they walked along the deck. She picked up her bag, dropped at the railside as she had fled.

At the top of the steps where the powerboat was moored, the skipper was waiting with some of his crew. As Sarah passed him alongside Bryce to go down the steps, he murmured with an innocent gleam in his blue eyes, "Goodnight . . . er . . . Miss Martindale . . . Mr. Taylor . . ."

"Goodnight, skipper. Have a good trip," Bryce replied lazily.

"And the same to you," came the subtle reply.

Down in the speedboat the oil boss swung Sarah aboard. In the gloom she watched him take the wheel musing to herself in humorous vein. She would have to start calling him Bryce. Soon now he would be her husband.

The engine roared. As they thundered away Sarah let her gaze rest on his dark shape with a loving, tender light.

Dear as he was to her heart, she would always think of him as *the oil boss.*

GOLDEN HARLEQUIN $2.25 PER VOLUME
Each Volume Contains
3 Complete Harlequin Romances

☐ VOLUME 37

ONCE YOU HAVE FOUND HIM by Esther Wyndham (No. 880)
Poppy Duncan spent Goodwood week in a beautiful Georgian mansion, with expense and luxury — under false pretences!

PLANTATION DOCTOR by Kathryn Blair (No. 682)
Doctor Sinclair thought that West Africa was no place for an unattached woman, but it was exactly the place for Lynden.

PARIS — AND MY LOVE by Mary Burchell (No. 565)
Marianne was young, she was in Paris and in love with Nat — but, so was the glamorous Lisette.

☐ VOLUME 38

SEND FOR NURSE VINCENT by Margaret Malcolm (No. 809)
Phoebe was thrilled on her return as district nurse to Rushford, but working with handsome Dr. Mellor did create gossip.

ISLAND FOR SALE by Alex Stuart (No. 614)
Although Alastair Macrae was forced to sell his precious land to the lovely American, he himself was not for sale!

WINTER IS PAST by Anne Weale (No. 582)
After five years Alex returned to the Malayan bungalow that was her home, and now her only link with the past was a forbidding stranger.

☐ VOLUME 39

SO DEAR TO MY HEART by Susan Barrie (No. 572)
When Virginia Holt accompanied her sister Lisa to Switzerland, she could not guess that her fate too would be decided by a famous surgeon.

THE NURSE MOST LIKELY by Kate Starr (No. 679)
Everyone thought that Hannah was indeed the nurse most likely to succeed — except Doctor Gideon Croft.

WHISPERING PALMS by Rosalind Brett (No. 731)
On their failing tobacco farm in Africa, the Nortons are not prepared for change, especially the dictatorship of Fernando del Cuero!